THE GHOST
AND THE DARKNESS

Patterson dropped to his knees for the shot. Starling did the same. And as they both raised their rifles, the pale lion growled louder and, moving fast, pulled the body deeper into the shadows at the far end of the station.

Patterson sighted down the barrel at the back of the beast, found his aim, and was about to fire when Samuel cried out and pointed back toward the roof of the station above them.

A black shadow was suddenly there, this monstrous dark thing that appeared suddenly from the flat-roofed part of the station and moved across the sun, actually blocking out its rays. Fully stretched out, it seemed to go on forever.

Patterson and Starling, turning simultaneously, saw the great length of the mysterious shape just as it launched itself. The enormous black-maned lion dove into the three men and sent them all sprawling. Then, with a deafening roar, it was off running across Tsavo station toward the white-maned lion.

The two lions stood and looked back at the men.

The Ghost had blood and chunks of flesh on its mouth. And the Darkness had crazed eyes that pierced the very souls of the onlooking men.

They were bringers of destruction, these two. They were able to kill the old and the young and the fat and the strong—anyone and everyone who came across their path.

THE GHOST
AND THE DARKNESS

A NOVELIZATION BY DEWEY GRAM

POCKET BOOKS

New York   London   Toronto   Sydney   Tokyo   Singapore

An *Original* Publication of POCKET BOOKS

 POCKET BOOKS, a division of Simon & Schuster Inc.
1230 Avenue of the Americas, New York, NY 10020

Copyright © 1996 by Bernina Film Ag.

ISBN: 0-671-00305-4

First Pocket Books printing October 1996

10 9 8 7 6 5 4 3 2 1

POCKET and colophon are registered trademarks of
Simon & Schuster Inc.

Printed in the U.S.A.

PREFACE

This is the most famous true story of Africa. It happened a hundred years ago, but even now, when children ask about it, you do not tell them at night.

Although the unmapped, mysterious interior of Africa was the main stage of the story, it really began elsewhere. It began in the great capital cities of nineteenth-century Europe, in the hearts of large-egoed, ambitious men eager to grab destiny by the throat.

Some of these were exemplary men answering to the highest ideals. Some were greedy scoundrels who saw the main chance.

John Henry Patterson was one of the former. On the night the story begins in earnest, he was on his way to answer a summons from one of the latter.

Horrors rarely known to man and acts of unspeakable bravery were just around the corner when these two men met. How were they to know what was coming? And if they had, would that have stopped either of them? Each, after all, was simply acting according to the dictates of his character.

The man of questionable character had much to gain: For all his crass ways, he was an empire builder.

Patterson had so much more to lose: He was the one going out there.

Patterson was witness to it all.

A fine man, yes. But do not become attached to him. There are many fine men in this story but do not become attached to any of them. So many of them die.

And remember this: Only the impossible parts of what follow are true.

Surrounding circumstances tended to vary in detail in the memories of survivors, and blurred from teller to teller. The main events, however, were confirmed by many, and they were as follows.

THE GHOST
AND THE DARKNESS

ONE

LONDON, 1898

A watcher looking down on The City—the business district in the heart of London—on a rainy night that winter would have seen a quarter bustling under the civilizing influence of electric lamps, thronging with commercial men buzzing on errands aimed at improving their lot and the lot of mankind.

Coming from far off, flying through the downpour and oblivious to it, one would have seen the tiny figure of a man in khaki uniform carving his path through the flowing horde.

The closer he came, the more he grew in stature. One could soon see that, far from tiny, he was a strapping character of ramrod bearing and long, purposeful stride.

The burghers he passed could see that underneath the flying oilskin slicker was the uniform of the British army, in perfect press and trim, brass polished, leather gleaming. The uniform bore, on the epaulets, the gold bar and four-pointed pip of a lieutenant colonel.

This fair-haired, strong-jawed, long-striding young man was Lt. Col. J. H. Patterson, late of the 5th Northumberland Fusiliers in India. He wore his fair hair cropped short around the ears and evenly shorn on top. The windows of his restless dark eyes revealed much about the man: seriousness of purpose, keen-mindedness, and a thirst for whatever demanding work or exhilarating adventure might be around the corner that very night.

Patterson was already, at his young age, a man of recognized talents and accomplishments. He had been summoned on this rainy night because his reputation suited him for an important and difficult job.

He turned in at an elaborately facaded building, identified on the embossed brass plaques on flanking pillars as the offices of the British East Africa Trade Association. A name to conjure with, as anyone active in colonial affairs of that era well knew.

Patterson pushed through the tall bronze doors, crossed the marble foyer, and immediately mounted the broad staircase leading to the director's office.

He strode down a high-ceilinged corridor in the elegant building, noting the lovely woodwork all around him. Everything was clean and in perfect order.

It was clearly after office hours, as many people were still leaving the building.

Patterson stopped at a large ornate door and knocked sharply. After a few moments, the door opened.

Robert Beaumont's office was a chamber imposing in its grandness and, thanks to the magnificently drawn maps and charts adorning the walls, instantly intriguing to one such as Patterson.

Maps and charts apart, however, the chamber was spare, utilitarian, and cold. Reflecting its occupant, Patterson was about to discover.

Robert Beaumont, director, founder, and chief strategist of the British East Africa Trade Association, opened the door himself.

At first blush he was a handsome, hale fellow, with a smile like the beacon of the Dover lighthouse shining from underneath a bushy mustache. He welcomed Patterson with a flash of his great smile and an outstretched hand.

"John Henry Patterson, come in," he said. "I'm Robert Beaumont." He shook Patterson's hand. "Firm—I like that, tells me a lot about you."

An altogether charming fellow, yes?

He ushered Patterson into the smoky room. Wall lamps were lit all around against the rainy darkness without. He gestured Patterson to a brass-studded, oxblood-leather armchair and walked around behind his great slab of a mahogany desk.

A clerk in gartered white shirtsleeves moved around the room, turning the lamps off one by one as the men talked—or, more precisely, as Beaumont talked to Patterson.

Patterson didn't mind in the least. He was an unflappable young man, secure in his own worth and self-perception, and was quite happy to let the older man talk and reveal himself.

Which Beaumont did swiftly and without any prompting.

"Now why don't you tell me about me?" Beaumont said. "To get you started, many people find me handsome, with a wonderful smile. I'm sure you agree."

A little surprised at the man's oddly vain gambit, Patterson gave an uncomfortable nod. Beaumont was about forty, he thought; the bespoke-tailored suit and heavy gold watch, watch chain and rings conspicuous testaments to his formidable prosperity.

"Winning personality, heaps of charm?" Beaumont went on.

Patterson cocked his head and looked this strange duck in the eye. "My wife is the game player in the family, sir," he said.

Beaumont gestured impatiently. "Games?" he said. He fixed Patterson in a deadly glare, leaning toward him. "Look at me closely, Patterson: I am a *monster*. My only pleasure is tormenting people who work for me, such as yourself." He flashed his brilliant smile again, only this time it was chilling. "One mistake and I promise you this: I'll make you hate me."

A wonderfully self-important son of a bitch, Patterson thought, marveling at the man's mercurial manner. He was evilly serious in his threats, Patterson guessed.

Beaumont turned sharply and moved to a large map.

The map.

Patterson had picked it out the moment he entered the room. "British East"—the vast concession called British East Africa carved out of the equatorial latitudes by the British East Africa Trade Association.

Etched on the map was a clear line that ran from the Indian Ocean coast at Mombasa inland to Victoria Nyanza—Lake Victoria—a distance of some 650 miles.

Beaumont, sweeping his hand along the line, said, "We are building this railroad across Africa for the glorious purpose of saving Africa from the Africans. And, of course, to end slavery. The Germans and French are our competition. We are ahead, and we will stay ahead, providing you do what I hired you to do."

He whirled and jabbed his index finger toward a more detailed map. It was a closer rendering of the railroad route, called the Uganda Line, but completed just to an area designated "Tsavo," 130 miles in.

"Build the bridge over the Tsavo River," he went on. "And be finished in five months time. Can you do that?"

Patterson rose from his chair and went to the maps. To him they were objects of perfectly sensuous delight. Beautiful linen-backed rectangles etched in colors rich and kaleidoscopic as the lands themselves.

Immediately he was a boy again, lost in the maps of Asia and Africa his army-officer father had brought home. Even now he was mesmerized by the poetic place names and the great blank areas in which no explorer had yet ventured.

The romance of maps was a big reason Patterson stood where he was at that moment. He had been actively drawn to those great blank areas with their inscriptions in fine ink: "Uninhabited Forest—Animals Unknown." "Great Impassable Gorge." "Pagan Tribes." "Impenetrable Swamp—Malarial Fever." He lusted to cast his eyes on animals and plants without names, to see for himself the cataracts that touched the sky and the mountains so high they bore snow at the equator.

He scrutinized the Uganda Line map lovingly as Beaumont repeated, "Can you do that?"

Patterson answered, his back still to Beaumont, "I'm sure you've examined my record, so you know I've never yet been late on a bridge."

5

"I'm aware of your 'glorious' record, Mr. Patterson," Beaumont said, "but may I humbly remind you that you've never built in Africa."

"But I have in India," Patterson said. "I expect problems."

"You'll have plenty of them. It's a wilderness," Beaumont said. "You'll be on your own over there. Don't come running to me for help."

"I like the wilderness," Patterson said evenly, turning to face the intentionally tactless Beaumont. And, dealing from the same deck, he gave as good as he got: "There are no bureaucrats, sir."

Beaumont nodded curtly, unfazed by Patterson's bravado. "You'll need your confidence, I promise you," he said.

Patterson sauntered away from the map, sizing up the rest of the room as the obsequious shirt sleeved clerk moved from sconce to sconce around the walls, extinguishing the lamps. "I've got a reason far beyond confidence," Patterson said. "I've just found out my wife is having our firstborn in six months, and I promised I'd be with her when the baby comes."

"Very moving, Patterson. I'm touched you confided in me," Beaumont said, lighting a cigar without bothering to offer one to Patterson. "But I don't really give a shit about your upcoming litter. I've made you with this assignment," he added with a bland smile. "Don't make me break you."

Patterson was not intimidated. He was now certain he had this man's number: the insistent rudeness designed to instill in an underling a subservient eagerness to perform. It was an act wasted on Patterson, who performed to meet his own exacting standards,

6

which were tougher than any employer could ever impose. He smiled blandly right back. "You won't have the opportunity," he said.

"You're not English, are you, Patterson?" Beaumont said.

Patterson shook his head no. He was the only child of Irish parents who took him out to India with them when he was a boy.

"Pity," Beaumont said blithely. Another crude attempt to make Patterson feel puny, and eager to come up to this worthy Englishman's standards.

"Any more words of encouragement, sir?" Patterson said, pushing straight on before Beaumont had a chance to carry the inane duel any further. "Then I've a train to catch," he said brusquely.

They looked at each other for a moment in silence in the near darkness of the office, their mutual disdain very clear. Patterson turned, picked up his oilskin, and marched out through the grand ornate door without another word.

TWO

Patterson, hurrying away through the rain, was keenly aware that there were broader issues underlying this railroad-constructing, bridge-building enterprise.

Beaumont had made it sound like little more than a sporting competition with the Germans and French. "We are ahead, and we will stay ahead, provided you do what I hired you to do," he had said.

This talk of competition, along with the other reasons Beaumont gave—save Africa from the Africans; bring an end to the barbarous slave trade—was shorthand, Patterson knew, for the exceedingly high-stakes international game being played out by nations on two continents.

This was no mere commercial job for a private trading company. The British army had not agreed to loan out one of its crack engineers to Robert Beaumont simply for that arrogant fool's aggrandizement. Nor had the British Foreign Office itself suggested and expedited the loan of Patterson out of paternalistic good will. This was a matter of state.

In fact, an absurd amount rode on the outcome of the contest going on in East Africa. East Africa, it was said, was the key to British imperial ownership of a whole continent.

Patterson hurried down the wet streets of The City with the heady feeling he was living on the cusp of events.

And he was indeed. This was the culmination of the era of European empire building. And in historical terms, Africa had just come on the trading block.

For centuries, the Gold Coast, the Ivory Coast, and the Slave Coast of Africa had been well known to Europeans. But the vast interior of the continent was still Darkest Africa, the subject of great fear and romantic speculation.

Unknown and exotic, enticing and threatening, it was *Terra Nullius.* Like America when Columbus sailed, Africa had no government and was considered to belong to no one, fair game to the first "civilized" parties to penetrate the land and stake a claim.

Growing up in India, Patterson had devoured the stories of Burton and Speke and the handful of other explorers, adventurers, and missionaries who went into the unknown interior first. Now within his own generation, the dogged foot soldiers of private enterprise were following.

H. M. Stanley, the *New York Herald* journalist who "found" the not-so-lost missionary David Livingstone, was one of the new foot soldiers. While tracking down Livingstone in central Africa in 1871, he saw the bigger prize all around him—a land rich in unmined treasures.

Livingstone went back to Europe and hustled up King Leopold II, king of the Belgians, as his backer and returned to a ripe and waiting Africa a few years later. He established the International Congo Association and set about developing the central African basin for the export of rubber, ivory, and whatever other unforeseen riches might be unearthed.

In a frenzied rush, trading companies from many European countries raced in and bought or strong-armed concessions from local tribal chiefs throughout Africa, establishing commercial beachheads. These cheeky entrepreneurs and traders, it turned out, were the stalking horses for Empire.

European governments gradually awoke to the opportunities and took over, transforming their nationals' trading concessions into protectorates and colonies. That was exactly what was happening with the British East Africa Trade Association. Patterson had been thrown to the fore in the march for empire.

He was of mixed feelings about the whole idea of empire and Crown colonies, but he relished the high stakes. He craved the chance to participate in events of great moment, to test himself in the fiercest arena his time had to offer. He possessed the immortality of the young.

Even before going in to meet with Beaumont, he had had the brashness to book passage for a journey to British East Africa. The sooner he got there to do this job of work for God and country—and do it surpassingly—the sooner he could return for his next triumph, the birth of his first child.

He hailed a hansom carriage and headed straight for Victoria Station.

THREE

The vaulting rococo framework of Victoria Station glistened and dripped under the evening rainfall.

A carriage pulled up and stopped beneath the archways. People were running back and forth; luggage was being unloaded. Amidst this welter of activity and tumult of noise, Patterson got out of the carriage and looked around anxiously.

Helena Patterson came hurrying through the crowd. She was a serene, natural beauty in her early twenties. She was still slim for a mother to be and she had not begun to show.

She fought her way through a tide of travelers and porters, looking fearfully this way and that. God forbid she should miss a goodbye. This was not their first, and she prayed, as she prayed every time he went forth on a posting, that it would not be their last.

She spotted Patterson and lit up in the smile she had for him only, running straight into his arms. "Tell me about Beaumont," she said brightly, practiced now at hiding her fears and heartache from her husband. "Does he understand how brilliant you are, and how lucky he is to have you?"

11

Patterson embraced his wife feelingly and, with a gentle smile, said, "It was embarrassing—the man showered me with praise."

They started to walk hand in hand under the archways of the building toward a quieter place. Patterson became suddenly very serious.

"Oh dear," Helena said, "you're getting that downtrodden look again . . ."

"I would never have taken this if we had known sooner," he said.

"And you would have been in agony and it would have been my fault," she said kindly. "You've been desperate to see Africa your whole life."

"What if there are complications?" he said.

"Not *'what if.'* There *will* be," she said, "there always are. Which only means that our son and I—note my confidence—will have an excuse to come visit."

The train whistle echoed through the cavernous station.

Patterson jerked his head up at the sound like a fire horse throwing up his head at the sound of the bell. In his mind he was already halfway to Africa. "Come along," he said. "Put me on the train."

She stood her ground, afraid to go with him as far as the platform, afraid her strength would falter should she actually have to see him step onto a departing train. "You go," she said, composing a smile. She turned to leave.

Patterson took her hand, tugged her back, and sweetly kissed her hand.

"Such a gentleman," she said with a sad smile.

Then he held her, taking her a couple of steps far-

12

ther away from the entrance. They hugged passionately, prolonging the inevitable separation.

"I don't have to leave," he said.

She held on to him, hating the moment, hating the reality. "You build bridges, John," she said. "You've got to go where the rivers are."

They held each other a moment longer, then broke apart, only to embrace each other a final time.

Patterson then ran to the top of the stairs. He turned to look back at her as a cloud of steam enveloped him.

FOUR

Even as Patterson's train sped out of the city and he settled back to read the *Times* of London, it was borne in on him that his mission was at the center of a gathering storm. The headline glaring out at him from the lead story was "Friction Among Great Powers over African Question at Combustion Point."

Patterson took it in stride. He was an engineer but also a student of history. Having been raised in Ireland and India, he was a child of Empire, and as a schoolboy he had followed the first stirrings of interest in Africa.

His army-officer father had required his son's presence at political discussions on the stifling veranda of their hill-station home in northern India. The senior Patterson and his army colleagues would pass the evenings hashing over the issues while monsoons blew through the oak and bamboo forests outside.

The logic of African empire building had been—rightly, they all agreed—rejected out of hand by the level-headed governments of the European Great Powers; Germany, France, and Britain. The usual arguments for empire—to open new markets, provide

outlets for emigration, create opportunities for invest-
ment of capital—just didn't apply in that savage land.

But gradually, thanks to small groups of imperialist
zealots, a kind of colonizing fever took hold and swept
Europe—a sense that this was a historical moment not
to be missed. If a country did not grab a chunk of this
virgin land mass now, it would forever lose out.

Patterson's father and his fellow officers fell into
two implacable camps over the issue, and the debates
grew into vitriolic shouting matches.

That tempest in a remote colonial teapot mirrored
the larger conflicts at home, from which a mad imperial scramble ensued.

Germany grabbed. In short order, it had established
colonies in both west and east equatorial Africa, eventually pushing to unite a belt of German colonies all
the way across the equator.

France set about establishing its own east-west
swath of colonies, from Saharan West Africa to Aden
on the Red Sea.

The pro-empire forces in Britain promoted the notion of an uninterrupted north-south corridor of British colonies stretching from Cairo to Capetown. East
Africa, lying halfway between and along the equator,
had long been the linchpin in this grand British design.

Patterson was steeped in the politics of it all. He
was vividly aware that the pressure to complete the
empire was ferocious, and that the rivalry among the
Great Powers was growing increasingly bitter.

Patterson realized he was marching into a cauldron
and, by God, he embraced the opportunity.

FIVE

MOMBASA

Lt. Col. J. H. Patterson landed by steamer at the port of Mombasa on the south coast of the East Africa protectorate in the early spring of 1898.

It was a green and inviting place when one approached through the narrow harbor filled with the picturesque coastal dhows and native fishing dugouts. A former Portuguese holding now in Arab hands, Mombasa was an island joined to the coast by ferries and bridges. Its giant spreading baobab trees, towering coconuts, and whitewashed building fronts cast an air of tropical splendor over the city.

Patterson, however, student of African that he was, knew modern Mombasa to be, even at this late date, a corrupt and dangerous city rife with slave traders, thieves, and pirates. Its colorful mangoes and flamboyants disguised a venal reality.

He disembarked, hired a *gharri* to transport his baggage, and set off at a fast pace, the fiery midday equatorial sun be damned. He made his way through the dusty streets and the flowing crowds of Arabs, Portuguese, East Indians, and native Swahili, turning aside all entreaties and offers of exotica of a material and fleshly nature.

He marched to the railway offices of the Uganda Line on the far side of the city, there to book passage inland on the earliest possible train.

Just as he finished purchasing his ticket, a young man wearing ill-fitting clothes, and with an unruly mop of curly black hair, presented himself to Patterson. "You're the new bridge-builder, yes?" he blurted. He did not wait for Patterson's nod to stick his hand out. "Angus Starling," he announced in a thick Scottish brogue; pumping Patterson's hand. "I'll be assisting you at Tsavo."

Patterson was about to answer the young man when Starling suddenly yelled out to a porter who seemed to be taking Starling's luggage in an opposite direction. "Excuse me for a moment," he said, and was off like a shot, calling over his shoulder to Patterson, "I will catch up to you on the train!" Patterson smiled to himself as he boarded the train, his thoughts turning from the amicable young Starling to the voyage ahead.

The "civilized" coast of Africa was of no interest to him. He had had his fill of meretricious and decadent Oriental cities in his travels with his father and later with his own engineering postings. The interior was where his imagination had already leapt.

When the train pulled out of the station the next morning, headed north up the fertile littoral, then west away from the coast and into the mysterious heart of the land, Patterson was occupying the only seat he would agree to use.

For his first glimpse of real Africa, he wanted the view to be unencumbered. He sat alone on the engine seat—a bench mounted in *front* of the train engine, forward of the front wheels, right over the broad cowcatcher. It was mostly used by train inspectors and intrepid visiting VIPs.

Deafened he might be by the constant pounding and bellowing of the steam locomotive. Blinded he might be by the ubiquitous billowing clouds of grit and dust. But there he would perch as the train roared away from the known margin of the giant land toward the unknown. There he would journey, happy and expectant as never before in his life.

Coconut palms and dense coastal vegetation gave way quickly to the forested uplands of the Rabai Hills. Patterson was all eyes and ears. Then, just as quickly, the forest gave way to the scrub-covered Taru Desert and more fine dust. A monotonous, bleak landscape that would stretch on, it turned out, nearly a hundred miles inland.

Patterson, his first misconception and his first disappointment with the new land under his belt, retired to an inside coach to enjoy the ride on the finished portion of the fine and already famous Uganda Line.

At that moment in Britain, the opposition were singling out the Uganda Line as the "Railroad to Nowhere" and the "Lunatic Line." Backbenchers in Parliament predicted this particular grand venture into the African wilds was an enterprise of fools that would exhaust the treasury and yield nought but national disaster.

But the tide in Britain was definitely turning strongly in favor of empire. The slogan "Africa British from Cape to Cairo" had gripped the popular imagination and become an anti-French and anti-German rallying cry.

Along the whole length of Africa, British prestige,

18

troops, and resources had been committed to the dream of conquest. The Dark Continent was a pearl of great price. No one could say what future riches lay in the inexhaustible interior.

Germany, in German East Africa just to the south of British East Africa, was surveying its own rail line to Lake Victoria and the interior. They wanted the treasures of the lake region and of landlocked Uganda to the north, so far unclaimed, for themselves.

In the Sudan, a would-be British possession just north of British East Africa, France had hunkered down for a showdown. The French had decided to stop the south-ward imperial thrust of General Kitchener and his aide, young Winston Churchill, who were marching up the Nile into the Sudan out of British Egypt. French and British forces were at this very moment at the brink of war at Fashoda on the upper Nile.

Britain was already at war elsewhere in Africa. Cecil Rhodes, the British prime minister of the Cape Colony at the southern tip of the continent and a principal author of the Cape-to-Cairo dream, had earlier pushed northward into Rhodesia. Now he committed the British nation to war with two small neighboring republics, the Transvaal and the Orange Free State.

Gold and diamonds were the prize and proximate cause. Their discovery in the Transvaal had put flesh to the bones of the idea that there were vast riches to be had in the conquest of the Dark Continent.

Curiously, Patterson thought, it was Bismarck who was the ultimate cause of *his* being a part of this whole circus. Thirteen years before, the German minister, disgusted with the shameful greedy antics of his European peers, called a conference in Berlin to draw up rules—an international code governing European acquisition of African territory. The code was a main reason Patterson was on his way out to Africa.

The international code required European nations to establish "real occupation" of any claimed territories. This meant there had to be in place actual colonies of settlers, or working governments administering the territory, or troops in occupation.

The first thrust for the British in establishing "real occupation" was the building of permanent transportation into the area—a railroad—to open the way for military occupation if necessary, and for administrators as well as commercial exploitation.

The Cape-to-Cairo dream depended on the belt buckle in the middle. And fastening that belt buckle depended on completing a railroad all the way across East Africa to Lake Victoria, and on to Uganda, before the Germans or French could push ahead and establish their own "real occupation."

The bridge over the Tsavo was just one link in a grand chain. But it was a key link. No stone and girder bridge meant no large troop movements, no transport vehicles or heavy freight, no parcels and mails, or any of the things that would signal "real occupation" of the interior.

Pretty sizable assignment for a young army engineer, Patterson daydreamed, staring out the window of the rail car. Just so, he thought. This was why he had joined the army in the first place. This was why he was a builder. To be at the very center of things. He had no fear whatsoever of what was coming.

SIX

At just over the hundred-mile mark, somewhere between the villages of Voi and N'dii, the character of the land changed to more agreeable rolling wooded hills. Patterson popped out onto the engine seat again, where he was immediately rewarded with the payoff of a boyhood dream: the sight of the snow-capped top of Africa's tallest mountain many miles to the south, 19,700-foot Kilima N'jaro.

A good omen, he thought. The Masai called Kilima N'jaro's western summit *Ngaje Ngai*—the "House of God."

He was basking in the spectacle of this legendary ice-topped giant just a few degrees off the equator, when suddenly there beside him, running like a madman to keep up with the train, was a skinny, gesticulating young man—Starling.

He was all angular arms and legs and big welcoming smile, trying to pull himself aboard the engine seat. If ever there was a physical opposite to the spit-and-polish Patterson, here he was. And yet Patterson sensed the man was a terribly appealing sort. As he gave the fellow a hand up, he was sure he was going to like him.

21

"Many thanks," the young man said, puffing for breath. Then, squinting at his seatmate, he asked, "So, I take it that Beaumont has already filled you in on all the paticulars about the bridge, yes?"

"He just gave me his 'monster' speech," Patterson said.

"Oh, that one," Starling said, tugging his sleeve down. "I know Robert seems dreadful, but when you truly get to know the man—well, he's much worse." He chuckled good-naturedly, tucking in his shirttail. "And I'm one of his defenders."

Patterson smiled. He was right: This man was impossible not to like.

"Forget him for now," Starling said. "It's your first ride to Tsavo. I think you'll find it breathtaking."

But once again, the steam locomotive chuffed out of the belt of woodlands onto arid plain. Patterson was treated to the pale yellows and browns of dusty, dry, thorny Africa. Especially more of the dust.

Starling coughed like crazy, hands over his face, which was becoming caked with a thick layer of grime. He and Patterson stared around at the bone-dry landscape. This was Africa, to be sure, but the one in Patterson's mind's eye was a landscape far richer with life, exploding with green, riotous growth that hid mysteries.

Patterson shouted to Starling over the noise of the engine, " 'Breathtaking' doesn't begin to do it justice."

Starling started to laugh, but as his mouth opened sand flew in, and his coughing fit doubled in its intensity.

The train, mostly flatcars and wooden-slatted freight cars loaded with construction supplies, labored up a

22

steep grade, and soon enough, the landscape began to change once again.

The train topped a rise and emerged in what seemed to be an entirely new land. And Patterson's face reflected the stunning difference. What he saw, at last, was the Africa of his imagination.

The desert had ended. Deep green and yellow grasses and lofty, swaying trees carpeted the earth, and bursts of animals appeared on both sides of the train. A flock of scarlet birds materialized overhead, and a cluster of tiny elegant Thomson's gazelles doing their amazing synchronized turns and leaps came into view.

Waterbuck and zebra grazed out on the savanna. Big-headed, blackish wildebeest, spooked by the sudden appearance of the train, bolted away from the tracks, sending a flock of sand grouse into nervous flight.

Patterson was like a kid in a candy store. He felt like a boy stepping into the pages of a Rider Haggard novel.

Starling pointed a slight ways behind the train. "Aren't they amazing?"

Patterson turned. What his companion was pointing at was a large family of giraffes running along, their absurd shape suddenly graceful as they ate up the ground in incredibly long, galloping strides.

Patterson and Starling stared in simple wonder, smiling at God's creation.

"You know the most amazing thing about them?" Patterson said. "They only sleep five minutes a day."

Starling glanced at him inquisitively. Clearly, he didn't know that.

The train passed an outcropping, behind which a family of hyenas, startled away from a kill, loped a few yards off in their sly, grinning way.

"Don't much like them," Starling said.

Patterson nodded. "The females are bigger," he said. "Only animal here like that. They have to be or they wouldn't survive, because the males eat the young."

Starling studied Patterson. Clearly, he didn't know that either.

Some hippos moved out from the shade of spreading baobab trees, doing a slow trot toward a narrow river winding near the rail line.

Starling turned to Patterson. "Anything special about them?" he said.

"Just that they fart through their mouths," Patterson said. "Must make kissing something of a gamble."

Starling laughed. "I've lived in Africa a year and I don't know what you know," he said. "How long have you been here?"

A contingent of big, ferocious baboons scattered off the tracks ahead and ran up into some rocks.

Patterson looked at his watch. "Almost twenty-four hours," he said. "But I've been getting ready all my life."

The train slowed down as a bunch of impoverished-looking native women herded sharp-ribbed cattle across the tracks. They held children who waved at the passing train. The children were thinner, more haggard looking than their mothers.

Touched by the sight of the youngsters, Starling shook his head. "Every time I see something like that," he said, "I know we're right to be here, to bring Christianity into their lives, enrich their souls."

"Beaumont says it's to end slavery," Patterson offered dryly.

Starling shrugged. "We all have our reasons," he said. "Mine is simply to make them understand happiness, accept salvation, know the serenity that comes ..." He stifled himself. "Best I stop. One of the byproducts of my belief is that I can become amazingly boring. But I know God smiles on me."

Patterson had to smile. "Have you got that in writing?" he said. Patterson could see that this Starling was, unquestionably, a good man. Morally impeccable, very much a product of the British missionary ethos and Victorian times.

Two lean, long-boned cheetahs vacated the rock outcropping where they had been snoozing, driven out by the fierce baboons, and dashed away from the huffing steam engine.

25

SEVEN

TSAVO

A white claw, was what Patterson thought of at first glance. Hundreds of white claws.

They weren't claws at all but sun-bleached thorns as sharp as claws, on a twenty-foot-high thorn tree.

And there were hundreds of these trees packed together, mixed in with other trees, low and stunted, and thick underbrush and baked red rocks.

The narrow-gauge track knifed through this forest of bone-white thorns, through a tight defile cut specifically for it. The train began to slow as it moved through the eerie briar patch.

Somewhere ahead, smoke drifted across the tracks from burning fields. The train emerged from the thorn jungle, and Patterson found himself looking out on a world alien to this pristine wilderness.

"Welcome to Tsavo," Starling said.

Tsavo railhead camp, the end of the line for the bridge builder. This was as far as the permanent construction had gotten. Beyond lay the broad river that begged crossing.

The camp itself was a minor city: dwellings large and small, a large centrally situated train station, tracks that looped past the station in a giant circle and returned to join the incoming line—in effect a turnaround that formed the mile-sized perimeter of the inner camp.

Men were visible everywhere, many hundreds of men, going about their work. White Englishmen. Brown East Indians. Black natives. All in their varied dress—troop uniforms for many of the Englishmen, Indian laborers in their long white flowing robes and tightly wrapped turbans, and natives in multi-hued earth-toned garments wrapping their torsos, carrying bundles on their backs and heads.

It was an encampment still under construction but substantial in every respect.

The train station, by far the largest building, had been built with timber and standard wood planking, and had a peaked roof and a broad plank platform. With the red, blue, and white Union Jack flying overhead, it could have been a rural train station somewhere in England.

A big green military-style peaked tent pitched nearby served as an administration building. Rows of smaller field tents housed the troops. Timber and corrugated iron mess huts fed the workers. Tin-roofed outbuildings sprouted here and there.

The Indian workers had erected their own white tepee-like dwellings in a series of tightly arrayed villages spilling well beyond the circumferential railroad tracks.

Guards armed with long repeating rifles patrolled the widow's walk of the train station and perched on all four sides of the high-scaffolded wooden water tower flanking the station.

What they were guarding against, Patterson wasn't sure. Perhaps they were there to fight off hostile tribes.

A haze of brown-red dust rose up from the frequent passage of donkey carts ferrying construction materials, accompanied by a steady cacophony of shouting in Hindustani, Swahili, and other tribal dialects.

Men were working everywhere, for that's what Tsavo was: a place for hard, manual work.

The train went slower still. Patterson stood, took off his safari hat, beat the dust out of it, and took in his surroundings.

No one stood idly around here, he was gratified to see. But, he noted with interest, no one looked particularly happy, either.

The dusty engine's iron wheels squealed and threw sparks as the train hissed to a halt in a release of steam.

Patterson and Starling stepped off the engine seat onto the wooden platform of Tsavo Station.

One man stood apart from the rest: That was Samuel. Patterson picked him out immediately—a tall, smooth-faced African of considerable bearing.

Samuel looked out of dark eyes that in repose were hooded and sad, and in action, Patterson would learn, were far-seeing and steady. His garb was a short-sleeved, rough brown tunic over a brightly woven shirt, and small clicking bones dangled from his long, looped earlobes.

He was an ageless Akamba, with, occasion permitting, a smile that could light the world. His head

28

was shaved except for a skullcap of close-cropped hair right on top, which gave him a monklike appearance.

Thanks to that singular hair trim, and the tall wooden staff he walked with, Samuel struck Patterson as a downright biblical figure.

Patterson would soon learn that Samuel was very much of the present world, a tribesman with two wives and eleven children back in his village, for whom he provided support.

From early contact with missionaries, Samuel had developed an unusual curiosity about the white man. He marveled at the European's odd combination of practical stupidity and astounding skills and learning. Over the ensuing months, Patterson would frequently have the disquieting sensation of being observed by Samuel as if by an anthropologist from an advanced culture.

Now Samuel was busily giving instructions in Swahili to the workers who were unloading the train.

"Samuel is the camp liaison," Starling said as the man approached, "and absolutely indispensable. The only man here everyone trusts."

Patterson asked under his voice, "Does he speak English?"

Samuel, having heard, gave a slight nodding bow to Patterson and said, "And very poor French."

Starling hastened to introduce them. "Samuel," he said with formality and respect, "meet John Patterson."

Samuel took Patterson's hand and shook it. "The bridge builder," he said. He gestured to the working men. "We have been getting ready for you."

"Excellent," Patterson said with genuine enthusiasm. "Could I see the bridge site?"

Samuel nodded and took a deferential step back.

"I've got medical supplies to deliver," Starling said. "Come along to the hospital when you're done." He started off toward the hospital tents.

"I will bring him, Angus," Samuel said, gesturing the way for Patterson to proceed.

EIGHT

They walked past the water tower toward the river and stepped off the tracks as an engine and two flatcars laden with Indian workers passed by.

"Where are you from, Samuel?" Patterson asked.

Samuel pointed. "That way," he said.

Patterson pointed the opposite way. "I'm from over there."

They walked along the tracks past one dry, dusty encampment of workers after another. His work force would number about five hundred men, mostly Indians, Samuel told Patterson—Punjabis, Pathans, and Sikhs.

They lived in widely scattered enclaves, Samuel explained, spread several miles along the river and back from it along the tracks to Tsavo Station and beyond.

The very spread-out nature of the living quarters would create havoc for Patterson in the course of later events, but now he had no inkling of such circumstances.

As they moved along, Samuel pointed out that a bunch of Indian workers who might have come from the same town back in their country might choose to live in one large cluster of tents. Hindus lived with Hindus, Muslims with Muslims. Sikhs also lived with their own.

African tribesmen set up their huts farther off, up and down the river or back in the bush. The Swahili were in one area, the Teita, Kikuyu, Nandi, Nyika, Kamba, in others.

Patterson passed an Indian tent area. "It all seems under control, Samuel," he said.

"Thank you," Samuel said. "If it is, it's a miracle."

They passed near the cattle-pen area with the section of Muslim tents just behind. The men were starting to eat. Far in the background, African huts could be seen. The workers were not looking very happy.

Samuel shrugged. "The truth is the workers just do not like each other at all," he said. "Obviously, the Africans hate the Indians. But the Indians also hate the other Indians. Some of them pray to cows, while others eat them."

Unsmiling workers studied Patterson as he moved by. Up ahead, some Sikhs were erecting tents, also not smiling.

Patterson had been forewarned that the worker situation in Africa was critical. Indian workers had to be imported, conflicts notwithstanding, because African laborers were not the sort to do the work. African tribesmen were not from money economies. They did not see the logic of continuous backbreaking labor in return for a minuscule wage of rupees or shillings or pence. They had very little use for money, and very little use for the idea of individual gain.

The railroad did employ as many tribesmen as it could for such labors as brush clearing, water and wood carrying, and cattle tending. The Africans were happy to be paid in wire, knives, or food. To hell with bits of metal or paper.

The workers actually building the railroad right of ways, laying the track and cutting the stone for the permanent bridge, were those imported from India, where they had done such work for the British for many decades.

Samuel took the new Bwana through the foundry toward the sawmill. Each place was filled with Indian workers in their white flowing garments and wrapped turbans with the fabric tail hanging down the side.

As Patterson passed, he gave the Indians a wonderful greeting in their native language. They just stopped and stared at him.

"Bring the leaders to my tent later on and we can talk, get to know each other," Patterson said to Samuel. "Perhaps I can help."

"You can certainly try, but it won't work," Samuel said. "Nothing works here. Tsavo is the worst place in the world."

Patterson looked at Samuel in surprise at the statement. He opened his mouth to make inquiry but was interrupted by a loud yell.

Standing on top of the water tower was an extremely powerful Swahili. He waved to Samuel, who waved back. It was Mahina, a headman or *jemadar*. Turbaned, wearing robes, he was deep black and his face was marked by tribal scars.

Patterson stared up at him.

Samuel pointed onward. "Come to the bridge," he said. He urged Patterson on and led him along the tracks to a spot on a bluff above the tree-shaded river-bank where the tracks stopped abruptly in midair.

Patterson and Samuel stood high above the rushing Tsavo River, an unusual African river that ran all year, fed incessantly by the ever-melting, ever-building icecaps of Kilima N'jaro far to the south.

Samuel gestured toward the other side of the river. He saw the bridge in his mind's eye, arching the swift-flowing Tsavo, connecting with some actual tracks that picked up on the far side.

Patterson could see that Samuel too saw all that was missing—the hundred-yard-long bridge that would carry the missing pieces of track. What a blessing this man would be, Patterson thought to himself; he thinks as I do, as a builder does when he sets out to throw up stoneworks and timbers to match the bridge that already exists in his mind.

Across the river, Patterson saw black smoke rising a few miles away.

"Advance camp is across there," Samuel said, indicating the smoke.

"How many workers?" Patterson asked.

"Three thousand laying track, even though your bridge is not yet built," he said. "Each day they move two miles farther away."

Patterson's job was to build the bridge, yes. But he also had to build "the permanent way," as it was known. That is, he had to shore up, rebuild, and fortify with stone, for thirty miles on either side of the bridge, all the roadbed, cuttings, embankments, and other temporary emplacements the advance track-laying crew was now putting down. It was a lot to do in five months.

Patterson jumped down from the track and scrambled down the steep bank to the river's edge. He stared at the space where the bridge was to be.

Samuel followed on his heels. "Did it look like this in your mind?" he asked.

Patterson shook his head. "This is more difficult," he said. He turned and looked back up the steep near bank, then at the far bank, and at the rushing water between—sinking the stone piers in his mind, spanning the gaps, his eyes bright as a lover's. This was his work, and he was excited about it. "But how wonderful that it's difficult, it should be difficult," he said. "What better job in all the world than to build a bridge? Make things connect, bring worlds together, and get it right!"

Samuel clicked his tongue in assent and walked away.

Patterson stared out at Africa.

NINE

The hospital was a sprawling, crowded series of interconnected, odorous tents, dim inside compared to the bright tropical sun beating down on the canvas.

Patterson, led under the flap by Samuel, glanced around. It's not bad at all, he thought. Of course there were some patients, injured or with fever. But like the rest of the camp he'd just seen, everything was working well, seemingly under control.

Angus Starling left the bedside of a patient and approached.

"Finish your tour?" he asked in his unfailingly affable way.

Patterson nodded. "And anxious to get started," he said. He indicated the three dozen occupied beds of the field hospital. "What is this, mostly malaria?"

"Yes," Starling said, "but their suffering is only transitory, once they accept God into their hearts."

"That's just vomitous talk, Angus," a man's voice boomed. "The poor bastards will get even sicker if you don't shut up."

Patterson and Starling turned.

Dr. David Hawthorne moved up on them, drying

blood off his hands with a towel. He was a sturdy sort with a trim peppery beard and short-cropped hair the color of iron filings. He was a tough, middle-aged, heavy-drinking man who hadn't been tactful in twenty years.

"I'm David Hawthorne, this is my hospital," he said brusquely. "And my advice to you is, don't get sick." Then abruptly he stopped himself, gesturing apologetically. "That was meant to be charming," he said. "Sorry. I seem to have lost the knack."

"You never had it," Starling said matter-of-factly.

"Angus and I don't like each other much," Hawthorne said irritably.

Samuel spoke to break the tension. "I am also liaison between these two," he said.

"Clearly you don't share Beaumont's vision," Patterson said to Hawthorne.

"This sham? Ridiculous. Who needs it?" Hawthorne said. "It's only being built to control the ivory trade, make rich men richer."

"Then why stay?" Patterson inquired.

Hawthorne shrugged off the question. "Who else would hire me?" He turned fast to Starling. "Beat you to it, didn't I?" He smirked. "Oh yes, almost forgot," he said. "Brought you a little welcoming gift."

He gestured to a nervous African man who approached them. One of the man's legs had been badly hurt and bandaged, and he was in serious pain.

"This is Karim," Hawthorne said, "one of my orderlies. Attacked by a man-eater earlier today. First incident of that kind here."

Patterson said nothing, just studied the wounded man.

Starling was incredulous. "A man-eater attacks and you're such a buffoon you almost forgot to mention it?" he cried.

"Well, he got away, didn't he?" Hawthorne said. He turned to Patterson. "Karim was riding a donkey not far from here when the lion sprang on them—donkey took the brunt of it—then just as suddenly as it appeared, the lion ran off."

Patterson listened intently, no emotion showing on his face.

Hawthorne was kind of enjoying the dramatic moment he had created, and began to lay it on. "I know it's your first day and of course you must be tired from the journey," he said, staring Patterson in the eye. "But what are you going to do about it?"

Patterson eyeballed him right back and said evenly, "Karim will have to show me where it happened. And of course, I'll need the donkey." He cast a look around the tent and half turned to go. "With any luck, I'll sort it out tonight."

He walked out.

An astonished Starling and a bemused Hawthorne stared after him.

TEN

In Patterson's tent, neat, oiled-leather vanity cases lay side by side on a makeshift dresser. Beside them, an ox-blood leather toilet kit had been placed next to a precisely lined up stack of books. Placed at right angles to the books sat an oval portrait photograph of Patterson's wife, Helena, and a photograph of an older couple, the man in army uniform—clearly Patterson's parents. A nicely weathered pipe and a tobacco pouch lay casually in front of the photographs. It looked like an advertisement from a men's gazette for the well-outfitted sporting Englishman.

Patterson, looking trim as usual in his crisp khaki field drills and high, waxed Norwegian boots, finished unpacking his matching Gladstones.

He completed the stacking of his underwear in neat piles on a shelf alongside an impeccable pile of pressed shirts. He still wore his high collar and tie; he had not loosened the tie even a fraction, despite the dust and muggy heat.

He looked altogether composed and military next to the unruly visitor—a sweating, open-collared, enthusiastic Starling—who barged into the tent carrying

39

his tea. It was teatime, after all, and Starling wanted to drink tea with the lieutenant colonel to mark his arrival.

Patterson hefted his mahogany rifle cases, placed them on a work table, and opened them. He lifted out the partly disassembled weapons from the tin-lined interior. While Starling sipped and talked, Patterson inspected his half-dozen rifles and shotguns to see how they had survived the trip, wiping them down and assembling them.

It was clear that Starling already felt Patterson was more of a friend than the dispeptic Hawthorne.

"I couldn't believe it when you said 'sort it out,'" Starling said. "As if it were the most normal thing in the world. Ho hum, what lovely tea, I think I'll bag a killer beast this evening, nothing much else going on anyway."

"Well, I'm responsible for everything that happens here," Patterson said. "If the men are terrified, the bridge won't get built."

"You said 'of course' you'd need the donkey," Starling said. "Why 'of course'?"

"We know three things about man-eaters," Patterson said, sighting down the single barrel of his Holland .303 sporting rifle, making sure it was oiled and ready. "First, they *always* return to where they've attacked before. Second, they're *always* old—they can't catch other animals so they turn to us. And third, they're *always* alone—they've been cast out by their pride because they can't keep up."

Starling, sipping his tea, was trying to hide his excitement. But at the same time he was a bit reluctant. "I don't suppose I could watch."

"Have you ever hunted?" Patterson asked him.

"Well, not exactly," the pious Scot said. "I've never been all that adventurous, but this sounds so exciting."

"Will you be able to be quiet?" Patterson said. He liked Starling's pluck.

Starling's eyes lit up. He stood up and went out, returning to his own tent, which was grouped near Patterson's and a dozen other British employees and orderlies.

ELEVEN

Patterson had the setting he felt he needed. A clearing in the Tsavo bush, a tree, the middle of the night.

And a slightly wounded donkey.

The donkey, lacerated on the haunch, dried blood caked down its leg, had its ears straight up and was turning them back and forth like searchlights. By the panicked look in the animal's eyes, it knew it was dinner.

Patterson had roped it loosely to a small tree in the clearing, bells around its neck. Whenever the donkey moved, the bells made a sound. A warm night wind blew through the thick trees that surrounded the clearing half a mile upriver from the railhead camp.

Patterson and Starling were seated uncomfortably in a tree on the edge of the clearing, twelve feet up in the air. Patterson had his sporting rifle cocked and ready.

Starling, initially thrilled to be part of the hunt, was now embarrassed, rubbing one calf. "I do hate to be a bother, John," he whispered, "but the cramp's getting worse." He pulled up his trousers to reveal a muscle in his leg, visibly knotted. "The pain is quite unbearable now."

Patterson didn't turn his gaze from the donkey. "Shhh," he hissed in a low tone.

"I'm sure you mean that to be comforting," Starling whispered, "but—"

Patterson hissed again sharply, cutting him off. "You'll have to deal with it, Angus."

"That is precisely my plan," Starling whispered urgently, "but back in my tent." He began to climb down.

Patterson, who had had some experience with man-eating tigers in India, grabbed him. "Understand something," he whispered. "You'll be dead before you can make it to your tent. They own the night."

Starling's eyes went wide. He gritted his teeth, shifted his position, and glumly obeyed.

An owl, perched above them in the tree, hooted constantly.

The night wore on. Animal sounds carried on the night wind: nightbird song, hyena barks and howls. The owl flew off to join another hooter for rodent hunting on the grassy plain.

Starling's cramp relaxed and he was able to straighten his leg and get comfortable.

He soon fell asleep.

So did the donkey, first letting his ears droop, then his head.

Patterson, however, stayed in exactly the same position, facing the clearing and the donkey, his rifle across his lap. Only his head and eyes moved, scanning back and forth.

The bushes behind the donkey shook just a little.

That was all—an almost imperceptible shake of leaves. Patterson saw it, and brought his rifle up.

The donkey was suddenly awake and scared, braying pathetically.

Then it all went crazy. The donkey screamed as a lion appeared from the bushes, a bearded male, and Patterson fired one shot, the sound exploding in the quiet night.

At the sound, Starling toppled from the tree to the ground, landing shocked but unhurt. He landed close to the lion, and stared at it, paralyzed, his eyes as big as millwheels.

The lion lay over on its side, and a tremor ran through its long lean body. It snorted out one breath and died.

Starling righted himself and climbed slowly to his feet, staring at the sizable beast amazed. "One shot . . ." he said, looking over at Patterson jumping down from his tree.

Patterson strode over and stared down at his kill, in truth even more amazed than Starling. He looked the creature over with evident appreciation for its sheer handsomeness, but equally for his great fortune in bagging it. "So that's what a lion looks like," he said.

Starling's jaw dropped.

TWELVE

In the cool of the African morning, Patterson came to the hospital area at Samuel's suggestion. He would not have done it this way, it was not his style. But already he trusted Samuel's instincts with these men. The workers needed to be impressed with the new *Sahib*.

The workers, Patterson well knew, would be the key to getting the job done. Well-intentioned, energetic workers could make any builder look like a master. The other kind of workers could make him the fool with very little effort.

A considerable contingent of Indian and African workers had gathered in front of the main tent at Samuel's behest, and more were filtering in. An undertone of excitement ran through the crowd.

Samuel's deep voice came from back in the throng, moving closer. "One shot," he could be heard saying, *"one."* He came walking out of the crowd, really quite enthused, gesticulating with his staff. It was the first time Patterson had seen the man's wonderful smile.

"Patterson has made the nights safe again," Samuel

said. As he walked, three workers came behind him carrying the long, splendid body of the lion.

Dozens more men came running in from all over to see the dead man-eater.

Samuel mimed shooting: "BOOM!" he shouted for the benefit of the growing crowd.

Starling watched the excitement over the carcass of the lanky beast, pleased and excited himself.

Patterson stood behind him, quietly taking it all in, not putting himself forward in any way.

A sour-faced Indian in a brick-red, rolled turban pushed to the front of the crowd. This was Abdullah, a big-shouldered leader of a substantial group of Muslim laborers, who skeptically watched the new Englishman's doings.

Hawthorne came hurrying up, stroking his beard in anticipation. He pushed through to the front, clearly amazed at the lion. He turned his amazement on Patterson.

"My God, you sorted it out," he said with a laugh.

Patterson had to smile.

All around him, Indian workers and natives watched him in a new way. Samuel's "one shot" had been an essential touch, lending the proper element of near-magical proficiency to Patterson's performance.

"*Shabash, Sahib!*" came a cry from someone in the crowd. "Well done, *Sahib!*" It was picked up and repeated as a chorus.

The workers clearly believed they could safely entrust themselves in Patterson's hands. He was now "*Bwana*" to the Africans, "*Sahib*" to the Indians, in actuality and not just in name.

46

THIRTEEN

In his tent at night, Patterson at last dispensed with the tie, loosened the high collar, and began his engineering drawings by oil lamp, possessed of the *most* sanguine outlook.

He had seen the magnitude of the job. It was demanding indeed, but altogether achievable in the time allotted if they got cracking.

He had looked hard at the human factor. It was thorny, but he had managed to work with worse labor situations in India—rival Hindu, Muslim, and Sikh sects who would just as soon kill as cast eyes on each other.

And he had vaulted the first stumbling block in short order: the man-eater. A touch of luck never hurt any project. The kill shot on that obliging beast was a good omen for luck to hold throughout the project and have him home for the advent of fatherhood.

Out in the bush, far from the reassuring halo of Patterson's hurricane lantern, circumstances were already conspiring against him.

Antelope, zebra, gazelle, buffalo, boars, and other

smaller game had been driven back from the Tsavo vicinity by the noise and the stink of humans, the cook fires of the ever-spreading worker encampments, the game-taking by Brit contract hunters and natives whose job was to bring in provender.

A tract of veldt for miles around Tsavo was no longer providing the kills it used to for predators. The big meat-eaters were hungry and ornery. The clean-up crew—jackals and hyenas who preyed on their leavings—were plain out of luck. Vultures rarely circled, with little reason to sail down for their lead-footed landings and shuffling, shameless scavengings.

The biggest of the predators could have moved off also, followed the prey deeper into the bush. But they were lazy and used to the Tsavo plain. It was *their* territory. There were many good places for the females of the pride to raise cubs. And they liked lying in the cool wind that blew off the river during the day.

And, more importantly, a seed was germinating in their small brains, planted there by an unfamiliar but appetizing new taste ...

FOURTEEN

A large drawing flapped in the morning river breeze.

Patterson held it high, standing on the temporary bridge. Narrow, rickety, and low to the riverbed, this bridge was just downriver from where the big permanent structure would be.

He held up his detailed depiction of the permanent railroad trestle against the backdrop of its actual location over the flowing river.

He had envisaged large stone embankments leading to it, and the three monumental stone pillars that would support it.

He stood with Starling and the massive Swahili he first saw atop the water tower the afternoon he arrived, Mahina. He had quickly discovered that Mahina was bright, a great worker, and a respected *jemadar*—clearly somebody to keep close at his side and apprised of his aims.

They studied the drawing, and no question, they were excited about the grand enterprise.

"All right, Angus," Patterson said. "You and Mahina will oversee the foundation piers." He pointed to their proposed location in the river. "There and there."

He rolled up the drawing and led them up off the temporary bridge to an open area between the embankment and a grassy field behind them. He moved close to the high grass and found a place to unroll the large drawing on the ground.

"The hardest part will be getting the piers built," Patterson said, kneeling over the drawing, "and for that I'm giving you twelve thrilling weeks."

Starling, faced with the pencil-and-ink renderings of the towering stone abutments, reacted with surprise. "Aren't we full of ourselves today?" he said, kneeling next to Patterson. "I think it's because of the lion."

"Possibly," Patterson said. He smiled, but he didn't back off his request.

"You know, I too have killed a lion," Mahina, standing above them, said softly.

"You have?" Starling said. "How many shots did you need?"

Mahina was almost embarrassed. He said, in an even softer voice, "I used my hands." He held his big hands out, palms out.

Starling looked at him to see if he was kidding. Mahina wasn't.

Starling turned again to the drawing of those formidable piers. "John, twelve weeks is just not enough time," he said.

"Angus, you'll just have to use your hands," Patterson said. He smiled and held his palms out, Mahina style.

Mahina grinned down at that. He started to reply, but his words stopped and his smile died. He just stared.

Patterson and Starling looked up from the drawing

of the bridge and noticed Mahina staring off. They stood to see what he was looking at.

What he stared at was the surrounding field of tall grass. Or so it seemed. Nothing appeared to be unusual about it.

Patterson watched the field of tall grass as it began to bend and sway in a fresh wind. He gazed in silence.

Starling followed his gaze.

Mahina stood frozen, his eyes locked on the field.

Abruptly, the field was making odd patterns, as if something unseen were moving through it.

Patterson watched quietly, no sound but the soughing wind reaching his ears. In the field, nothing was visible but the odd pattern that seemed to be making its way across.

Mahina and Starling stared. The odd pattern seemed to stop. Around it, the wind made different shapes of the grass.

As the wind continued to blow, Patterson continued to stare at the spot where the pattern stopped.

Mahina continued to stare too, except that he suddenly began to shiver, as if from cold.

FIFTEEN

Work commenced in earnest the next morning, well before the equatorial sun could take the freshness from the air.

Patterson struck the first blow, wading yards into the river. Accompanied by Mahina, he checked the current and depth of the water.

Starling, Samuel, and Abdullah watched from the bank as Patterson used his theodolite and laid datum strings and ran ropes to indicate pier footings, occasionally consulting his drawings. As he worked, Samuel translated commands to the workers for him.

Starling and Abdullah were dispatched to coordinate the workers who cut and cleared undergrowth, using machetes. Starling did his best and tried to help, but alas, he was a bit on the clumsy side with the heavy blade. Balance was a problem for him. But stay with it he did, and he soon began to be of real service, hacking and hewing like a Welsh coal miner.

A worker dropped an ax. The worker next to him grabbed hold of him and was about to punch him when Samuel, ever vigilant for worker unrest, separated them.

Mules clopped across the low temporary bridge carrying stones from the upriver quarry to the site. The dust swirled down from the banks.

Other workers dropped stone after stone into the river as footings for the piers that would be erected.

Patterson orchestrated the whole event from the temporary bridge, with Samuel close to him to shout translated orders.

In a tin-roofed survey shed, with his laborers moving slowly outside in the unforgiving midday sun, Patterson bent over his engineering drawings. Samuel was with him in the shaded hut.

The sound of raised voices made them look out to see. Abdullah, a Muslim, was locked in a shouting match with a peer who was Hindu. They glared at each other unyielding, then abruptly separated.

Patterson called out, "Abdullah!" and hurried to intercept him. "We're going to have enough trouble making schedule as it is," he said quietly to the furious, red-turbaned foreman.

Abdullah gestured toward the man he was arguing with. "All Hindus are lazy and stupid," he spat.

"Fortunately for this project," Patterson said, looking him in the eye, "you are not prejudiced. You can work with anybody." Before Abdullah could reply, Patterson added, "If the bonus for finishing is large." He gave the man a meaningful look. "And if we finish *on time,* Abdullah, your bonus will be *very* large."

Abdullah considered that. Then with a small, crisp bow he said: "All men are my brothers."

SIXTEEN

Patterson, resting in his shaded tent in the late afternoon after his unrelenting labors, appeared to be finding his footing in the strangeness of Africa. There were outward signs. Gone was the high collar and tie, and gone the army uniform. He was *Sahib* here, with or without the uniform, and the men knew it.

He had on his reading spectacles and was writing a letter to Helena.

Samuel approached the tent and stopped at the open flaps.

Patterson gestured him in.

He entered and, without a word, presented Patterson with a tribute—a necklace.

It was made from lion's claws to celebrate his first lion kill.

Patterson took it and admired the fearsome white talons. Was it a talisman against evil? Did a man take on a lion's own strength and ferociousness when he killed the beast and took his claws? With any luck, his own strength and resolve would see him through this African venture, but he was not one to foreclose any avenues to success.

He tilted his head to Samuel in gratitude. And with respect for the powerful thing, put the token in a prominent place on his carefully arranged bookshelf.

He returned to writing his letter.

Patterson stood alone at one end of the creaking temporary bridge after all the workers had gone. He looked across the gray-green, murky Tsavo, swift and full with spring runoff from Kilima N'jaro. His gaze wandered over the bluff on the opposite bank and the ongoing railroad tracks to the pale yellow-green savanna and deep green hills rising beyond it. And over the hills, a sky trailing the last red and gold streaks of sunset.

Dearest . . . It is so beautiful here . . . he had written to Helena. *All my fantasies fell short of what surrounds me. I truly love Africa. The work is hard and grueling, as work is always hard and grueling, but we are ahead of schedule. I suppose I was afraid before my arrival that the place would not live up to expectations. Except for your absence, I cannot find a single thing to complain about. I can't wait to show this country to you. . . . Love, John.*

SEVENTEEN

Patterson stood on the interrupted tracks above the river surveying his fiefdom, checking the work against his projections.

Progress had been made at a rate well within his plan. He had every reason for an energized optimism, a bounce in his step. Good exhausting work all the long day. Good sound sleep in the cool African nights that were musical with animal sounds.

Starling had been doing yeoman's labor running the sawmill. He oversaw the cutting of lengths of timber to be used for scaffolding, braces, and stringers between the mammoth steel girders coming by rail. Now he was guiding some donkey cartloads across the temporary bridge.

On the far riverbank, a chain of workers passed rocks bucket-brigade style into the river, building up the footings. Mule carts carried more rocks to the abutment site on the near shore, where masons chipped at the stones, driven on by the hovering Mahina.

In his workers, Mahina saw, there was not the same bounce as in the *Bwana*. Monsoon season was coming, bringing with it unbearably humid days and sudden long thundering rains. A season of fatigue was on them, Mahina observed. The rock work was especially unforgiving and exhausting.

Mahina, who never tired, began a Swahili chant. And here was the surprise—when Mahina spoke, it was always softly, but when he sang, the sound was loud.

A couple of other workers picked up the pretty chant. Now a few more joined in, making it prettier still, more melodic and rhythmic.

On the bank, the laborers put their backs into their work with a little more willingness and a hint of conviction.

Muscled workers lowered wheelbarrows of rocks on ropes toward the riverbank. Abdullah oversaw the operation, even joining in the song.

The groundwork for the bridge had begun to rise. Platforms for building the spans were being finished. Scaffolding for erecting the piers were being raised under Mahina's instructions.

Mortar was mixed and spread by the teams of Pathans imported from India for their specialized skills and experience working with stone.

A cut stone was hoisted into place on a pier.

Patterson, standing apart with Samuel some yards upriver, couldn't help marveling. "The foundation work is going very quickly," he said. He signaled for the hoist laborers to lift the next cut block of stone.

"Let us hope," Samuel said.

Patterson stopped working and looked across the

river. He saw movement in the grassy area on the far side. He got Samuel's attention and pointed.

A strange little man was rising slowly out of the grassy field.

He was a member of the Kikuyu tribe—powerful primitive men who sharpened their teeth to points, giving them a threatening, dangerous demeanor.

Now another Kikuyu warrior rose into view. He was soon joined by two or three more. They all stood there with bright eyes and sharp teeth and spears and black glistening bodies. All of them silently staring—and very clearly they were avoiding having to look at Patterson.

"Kikuyu," Samuel said. "They mean no harm.'

"They seem angry at me, or frightened," Patterson observed.

Samuel was silent for a beat. "They have a legend about a ghost in Tsavo."

"I see," Patterson said, "because of my white skin."

Samuel shook his head. "It's not that sort of legend, John." He stared at the menacing Kikuyu. "Do you know what *Tsavo* means? 'Place of slaughter.' "

Patterson watched the Kikuyu tribesmen. And they still would not look at him. But they did shake their heads, almost sadly.

Patterson glanced around at his workers, wary of any work-slowing influence. The men were returning to their tasks, outwardly unconcerned. They probably knew nothing of any such legend. . . .

Not a full day later the project suffered its first accident.

A selection of scaffolding collapsed; men lay injured. Starling was first to rush down into the river. He yelled up at Hawthorne, who shouted at some workers to bring stretchers quickly. The workers loaded the injured onto them.

Patterson watched from the other side of the bank.

Later that afternoon, there were very few men on the same embankment that had been teeming with them in the morning.

Work had been stopped.

Samuel had read the emotional state of the men and counseled Patterson to grant the rest of the day off, lest there be more accidents. Patterson went along with it, though unsure of why it was necessary.

In the evening, masses of workers gathered on the slope of the river and knelt in silent prayer.

It seemed an overreaction. There had been an accident and men had been injured, yes. But no one had died. It was a frightened reaction that puzzled Patterson.

"You must understand Africa," Samuel said as they watched the injured men's countrymen petition their gods. There were bad places where Darkness dwelled, Samuel said, and no one remembered why. Three such places lay nearby. One was the forests of Rabai. Another was a certain lake on Mt. Kilima N'jaro. And the third was Tsavo itself. "Do you remember what I told you on your first day?" Samuel said. "Tsavo is the worst place in the world."

Patterson the history student was now instructed in local annals.

The railroad route from Mombasa to Lake Victoria was largely an ancient caravan route. It followed the water sources all the way. Tsavo, a caravan water stop, had been a place of ill repute for as long as Arab traders in ivory and slaves had plied the route, Starling offered. Caravan leaders, using enslaved or paid native porters to carry ivory and other loads on their heads, detested the place. At Tsavo, invariably, one or two porters deserted camp, disappearing into the night and leaving their loads behind.

Native legend spoke of an evil spirit who lured men out of camp at night and drew them down to the river's edge, there to whisk them away into the mist-enveloped waters. Sandals would be found, or a loincloth. Nothing else.

Samuel, a modern, enlightened tribesman, had his own explanation. Hot sulfurous ethers rising from the red lava rock outcroppings around Tsavo unsettled men's minds, he believed. Once one left the vicinity of the river itself, Tsavo was revealed as a place of burning sun and evil smell. The greenness and flowering that followed the monsoons was just evil disguising itself, he said.

Patterson listened gravely. He had had to deal with superstition before in India, and he knew that no matter how far-fetched his workers' notions were, one couldn't just dismiss them. One simply had to show the men that his project was somehow immune.

EIGHTEEN

The steam locomotive labored through the thorn-tree defile and eased into the camp, pulling a flatbed with several huge steel beams on it.

Teams of turbaned workers unloaded the beams and carried them into the camp. They made their way to the long, thin-roofed forge on the river side of the settlement and delivered the beams to the iron-workers.

Within minutes, sparks were flying from the anvils as hammers pounded hot metal. Silhouetted through smoke, men worked on metal plates and fittings.

The bridge was out of its infancy, into a toddling stage, where legs were standing. Spanning the great distance between shores no longer strained the imagination.

Patterson, in his high Norwegian boots and civilian clothes, stood on top of the embankment with Mahina and Starling, watching with pleasure.

They watched forge workers carrying metal fittings to the bridge site, where rivets were being heated at the base of the pier. The red-hot rivets were taken up by men wearing gauntlets and tossed to metalworkers on the top of the scaffolding. The rivets were then pounded into metal plates.

A huge structural beam, supported by a gallows and tripod sheering, was gingerly maneuvered out from shore and eased down into place. Sleepers were pulled away as the beam was lowered into its permanent home.

Mahina, Patterson, and Starling looked at each other. The embankments and the foundation pillars were finished. The near part of the span was up, blocking out a stripe of sky. The three of them were flying, ecstatic over the progress.

They held their hands open, out toward each other, in Mahina's gesture. It had kind of become their password.

It was a big moment for them all.

Patterson was a born engineer.

He grew up relishing the big machines and structures of the modern age: dams, steamships, bridges, railroads. He loved trains, loved running his hand over the great curved iron boiler of a new steam engine, smelling the oil and the new metal.

He couldn't wait for the Tsavo bridge and permanent way to be finished, whereupon the railroad would be sending up the line four of the heavy, powerful new Class F locomotives. He had already decided that he would ride the first one across the Tsavo bridge.

His first engineering job in the army was as an apprentice doing right-of-way work on a railroad into the Hindu Kush in the far northern reaches of India.

Within eight years he had his first chief-engineer job: a single-span bridge in Srinagar. There he made his name in short order, by slinging a sixty-foot girder across a chasm using only native hoists, no modern derrick or block and tackle.

His father, whose spine was collapsing excruciatingly from cancer, shotgunned himself in the mouth just hours before Patterson got home to share the details of his triumph.

It was often this way, Patterson found, in his life. The close yoking of the fine and the horrible served to keep his grand sense of his own excellence from soaring too close to the sun.

He desperately wished his father were alive to see this beautiful strong bridge, though. The old man's eyes would gleam, he was sure.

NINETEEN

Not three hundred yards from the encircling rail-line periphery of the main camp, at the edge of the open bush, a fire burned in front of Mahina's tent area where the big man sat, exhausted, with other tired but happy men.

A cash bonus loomed in front of their drunken eyes. They sat around the fire and speculated on the number of rupees and the goods they would be able to buy in Mombasa or India.

Mahina stood and, for all his bone-tiredness, began to dance around the fire, humming to himself as he moved.

At the same moment at the inner camp, Patterson was getting ready for bed, putting out his fire and carrying in his writing table.

Starling and Samuel appeared carrying a drunken Hawthorne.

"All men are brothers!" Hawthorne shouted upon seeing Patterson, and he insisted on being set down.

Patterson laughed and brought out a good brandy to share with his brothers.

Mahina, stumbling with exhaustion and drink, went

into his tent and lay down with a giant sigh. Almost instantly he was breathing deeply, sleeping the sleep of the deserving.

In Starling's tent, the missionary–bridge worker turned out his lamp, half asleep already, and left the Bible resting open on his chest.

Patterson, in his tent, closed his eyes and gave his last thoughts to Helena and his child to be. If the child was a son, he would bring him out here to see this bridge when the boy was old enough. He would want him to know the magnitude of his father's accomplishment. Perhaps the age of seven. When *he* was seven, Patterson thought just before dozing off, he already knew he would be an engineer, a builder of wonderfully useful things. . . .

Mahina lay deep asleep on this exceptionally quiet night. He shared his tent with a dozen others and they were all sleeping peacefully. They lay on the floor of the tent, on canvas and rugs, heads together toward the center pole, feet toward the edges of the tent.

An observer looking down from the center of the tepee-like tent would have a hard time seeing Mahina, or anything for that matter in that circle of men, so dark was the night. All the men lay motionless, breathing deeply.

They didn't move, not even an inch. The steady breathing was the only sound. The hyenas, lying in wait out in the bush, were quiet for the moment. The cries of the colobus monkeys were missing for once. Not even the night wind was making its usual soughing complaint.

Not a damn sound.

And then two things happened in quick succession. Mahina's eyes went wide, and then he started to slide out of the tent, as if being pulled by some giant invisible wire.

At the sound of Mahina screaming, the other men in the tent awoke, staring around. Some of them just saw the last of Mahina as he slid out of the tent into the night as his terrible screams grew even louder.

For the other men in the tent it was like a bomb went off. They rose, spun, cried out, and stared in confusion at each other.

In the pitch-black night outside, Mahina's body slid along the ground. He was face upward and he was going at tremendous speed. And whatever the hell it was that was making this happen was something he couldn't conceive of, couldn't believe, even as he caught glimpses across his own body of something utterly nightmarish.

Up ahead were some patches of scrub. And Mahina, his body going faster than before and his cries weakening, disappeared into them.

Out in the bush, in the stifling airless night and the intense darkness, a watcher would have seen Mahina's body passing, and no sound at all coming from him now.

And no sound from whatever it was that was dragging Mahina. Just the limp body of the big man as it skimmed along toward a clump of dense bushes, coming closer, closer—knifelike thorn bushes, a high wall of them. And Mahina suddenly rose magically in the night, his body flying over the bushes, and he was gone.

TWENTY

It was early morning, and Patterson, Samuel, and Starling, their rifles held in front of them, raced along,
following the drag marks in the dirt and the huge animal tracks.

Patterson had not been roused, and was not told his
jemadar had been taken until well after daybreak, for
Mahina's tentmates had huddled in their tent in utter
terror until then.

Only in full light did they trust that the beast or
devil, whatever it was, was not still lying on its kill
within striking distance of the tent.

Even had Patterson and his cohorts been alerted in
the middle of the night, they would have only been
able to venture fifty yards or so into the bush at that
hour. No one in his right mind wandered around in
the African bushland in the dead of night with a lantern that as much as cried out: Easy prey—come and
get it! Many iron-jawed creatures prowled the landscape, ravenous in the night hours, ready to pounce.

Suddenly Patterson stopped, staring down at the
dirt. At first it didn't look like much. But on closer
examination, he saw a spot of red.

Patterson, Starling, and Samuel hurried on again.

At the impenetrable wall of thorn trees, they stopped, looked, and found bits of garment torn off by the thorns. They forced their way through them and raced up the hill on the other side.

They saw *something* in the shadow of some big rocks, but they couldn't make it out. Lions? No. But before they could identify it, the something was gone.

The men pressed forward, moving through an area of giant rocks that looked eerily like teeth. They hadn't spotted what it was they saw yet.

Then a harsh sound erupted behind them, and Patterson, Starling, and Samuel spun around.

Vultures! Their great necks stabbed forward from the shadow of the rocks toward a shape the men couldn't quite make out.

But there were specks of blood all around on the rocks and the scrub.

Patterson, crying out in shock and fury, fired his rifle and raced forward.

The vultures, screeching and screaming, waddled madly and took off. As they beat heavily into the morning sky, Patterson saw the kill scene. There was barely a body left. Shreds of flesh and bone were strewn all over. And separated from the body, Mahina's head lay turned upward, his terrorized eyes staring at them.

The killer was long gone.

In the hospital tent, the walls flapped violently as lanterns were lit against the approaching squall outside.

Hawthorne, emotional, but trying to be professional,

talked against crashes of thunder. "What the lion must have done, once he'd killed Mahina," he said, his voice quavering, "was lick his skin off—here—so he could drink his blood."

He stopped in his examination of the body, trying to take hold of himself. What had been Mahina was ghastly.

Samuel was watching intently along with Starling, who was visibly upset by the grisly remains.

"Then he feasted on him," Hawthorne continued, "starting with his feet. Lions don't eat this way. Are you sure this was a lion?"

"We followed his tracks," Patterson said.

They stared at the pitiable remains on the table.

"What sort of lion could carry off someone Mahina's size?" Starling asked.

TWENTY-ONE

In the Muslim area of the Tsavo camp at sunset, red flames rose against the last of the dying sun.

Then it was just the red flames of the funeral pyre in the darkening sky.

Abdullah, his big surly face running in tears, swayed slightly back and forth. Many workers in white robes and turbans came to pray at Mahina's funeral. Men who had worked under the *jemadar* on the embankment or lived with him in his tent or knew him from rough joking at the supply stores came to grieve.

Samuel was there too, standing with Starling and Hawthorne. Patterson stood at the rear, terribly moved. He wiped away tears for a man he had come to view as a friend. Then, unseen by others, he held his hands out in Mahina's gesture one final time.

The flames continued to rise....

It was nearly night and Mahina's tent stood just as it had before, except that the tent flaps that were open when Mahina was alive were now closed and tied.

Patterson, lit by the distant flames of the funeral fire, climbed alone into a nearby tree, rifle in hand.

Man-eaters always returned to where they attacked before. It was the first axiom of lion or tiger behavior, and Patterson would be ready. He would avenge Mahina's death swiftly, though it would be scant recompense for losing so admirable a friend and workmate.

A bunch of silent workers moved past, hurrying to their tents in the deepening darkness.

Patterson managed to find a place to sit on a narrow but sturdy branch of the tree. He had a clear view of the tent itself.

Anger fueled his resolve. He would not leave that spot until the killer was bleeding on the ground.

Patterson was alone in the middle of the night, fifteen feet up in the tree near Mahina's tent. He held his rifle, ready for anything. He had good sight lines of the kill area. He could not, however, get comfortable.

In the area around Mahina's tent nothing stirred.

Rain beat down on Mahina's tent. The night stretched on. In the tree at the edge of the clearing, Patterson sat as before, guarding his clear sight lines, in the pouring rain. Lack of comfort was not going to throw him off course.

Rain would not stop a lion, and it would not stop him. A man-eater who found ready prey one night *would* come back the next night. Patterson was certain of it.

Still there was no sign of movement of any kind in this now-deserted area of the Tsavo camp. Just dead calm.

The rain had passed, the moon was lower in the

sky. The night was growing to a close, but still the darkness surrounded Mahina's tent.

Patterson, iron-willed and convinced he was right, looked forward to the misty first light of dawn, for predators liked the gray hour too. Predators knew that then, as at dusk, game moved easily, grazing, feeding in the half light and cool air.

At dawn, Patterson was still in his tree, unbudging. He battled fatigue, holding his rifle at the ready. But then, for a moment, losing the battle, his eyes started to close against his will. And as they did, one huge yellow eye appeared in the gray light.

That's all that seemed to be there, just the glinting eye. It was near Patterson's tree and it was staring up at him.

Patterson, startled, grabbing his rifle more tightly, stared down at the corner of Mahina's tent. Something was there. He had seen it, he was sure.

The huge yellow eye—only it was gone.

Patterson blew on his hands, looked toward the sky. The sun was rising, the night gone.

TWENTY-TWO

In the morning light, Patterson left Mahina's area at the edge of the bush and walked back toward his tent area. He was wrinkled and wary, frustrated and sore.

He stopped at the equipment warehouse. Gathered there were a large bunch of Abdullah's workers. Only right then they were not working. They sat, smoked, played cards.

Abdullah and Samuel stood nearby, face to face, arguing in Swahili.

"Watakwenda kanini nikiwaambia," Abdullah said with anger, his red turban shaking. "They will go to the bridge when I tell them."

"Lakini kukaa hapa haifai. Unajua hivyo," Samuel said. "But sitting accomplishes nothing—nothing at all—and you know it."

Patterson came streaming up. "Why is no work being done?" he said.

Abdullah gestured around. "Malaria epidemic. Very sudden," he said.

"Let me see the sick," Patterson said. It had been

73

the same in India—the sudden convenient malaria epidemic.

"Oh, you're a doctor now too?" Abdullah said insolently, not backing off.

Patterson stood his ground too. "There is no reason for fear," he said firmly.

"On that I choose to remain dubious," Abdullah said. "Two are dead now in two nights."

Patterson looked from Abdullah to Samuel, rocked. Two? That was news to him.

Behind him, Starling hurried up.

"A second death?" Patterson said to Starling. "Where?"

Starling gestured. "Far end of camp. *Mpishi*, native cook wandering alone at night," he said. "Hawthorne's examining the body now." He grimaced. "There's even less of him than of Mahina."

Patterson turned to Samuel in disbelief. "The lion should not be that hungry this soon," he said.

Samuel nodded. "We should construct thorn fences around every tent area," he said, quickly thinking what would placate the workers. "Bigger fires burning at night."

"Fine. Get started," Patterson said. "And a strict curfew—*no one* allowed out at night." He turned to Abdullah. "Send half your men to the bridge, the rest with these two."

Abdullah gave a begrudging nod, somewhat mollified by Samuel's remedies.

"We'll get this settled," Patterson said. "There is no reason for fear. I will kill the lion and I will build the bridge." He started to walk away.

As he left, Abdullah said for the others to hear,

74

"Of course you will—you are white, you can do anything."

Patterson overheard his remark. He turned to him. "It would be a mistake not to work together on this, Abdullah."

They looked at each other with a new hatred.

TWENTY-THREE

There was a use for everything in Africa, a native saying went. Every animal was food for another. Every plant fed or clothed or protected someone in creation.

Samuel now made it true for the *nyika,* the impassable thickets of twisted dwarf thorn trees.

Short, curved, black cutlasses in the hands of African workmen hacked at the endless forest of clawed vegetation. Under Samuel's direction, the Africans showed the Indian workmen how to attack the brittle, menacing growth without slicing themselves into bloody pulps.

Starling, not afraid of any tree, was not hanging back. He was taking less care than the others, swinging away with his machete, moving in between bushes.

Transported to the Muslim area, the thorn trees began to find their use. A boma fence was taking shape.

Starling, in charge of the thorn enclosure that was halfway finished, worked like a Trojan, strangely oblivious to injuries inflicted by the thorns. His clothes were shredded; his hands were bloody. His workers finished with a section and, satisfied with the work, moved on.

Samuel watched from the background as Starling charged in where the workmen left. He was far from finished. He grabbed the thorns with his bare hands, squeezed them together. "Not good enough," he said. "Look, it's got to be tighter. *Tighter.*"

At day's end, the entire inner camp and many of the outlying worker enclaves—which had been pulled in closer to camp—were enclosed by thorn palisades. The place was filled with fences now, all the individual areas protected.

The skies were starting to darken—dusk was coming fast. Fires started up. Dozens of them.

Then workers came racing home to their camps, anxious for safety before darkness took over. They zigzagged this way and that, dodging past each other, sometimes slamming into each other, falling, getting up, running on.

The sun fell out of the sky. Dead silence blanketed the common areas of the settlement. Not a single human ventured abroad.

TWENTY-FOUR

Gigantic fires leapt up from worker strongholds all around Tsavo, sending lurid columns of sparks high into the night.

Predators could have been stalking the dirt paths of the settlement unmolested. No one moved outside the rings of safety the fences provided.

Starling, in the main tent area, was bathing his bloody hands. Samuel was sitting near him, his own big hands unmarked. He withdrew a leather packet from the pouch he wore and passed it to Starling; an unguent for his wounds. He leaned back and closed his eyes. Both men were exhausted.

Patterson brought them each drinks. They nodded thanks and drained them. They sat there together, lit by the flames of their fire. The quiet way in which they attended to each other's needs and went about tending to their own underlined how close the men had grown together.

"What a good day," Starling said, salving his cuts.

"You mean nobody died?" Patterson said.

Starling shook his head. "We all worked together," he said. "Worthy deeds were accomplished." He smiled. "I liked the labor." He applied Samuel's balm and wrapped a poultice around one bloody palm. "My mother insisted on piano lessons—broke the dear woman's heart when I turned out to be tone deaf— but she still was always at me about being careful with my hands." He looked up at them. "I like the blood, is that so strange?"

Samuel didn't hesitate: "Oh yes, I think so."

Starling flashed his beneficent smile, the one that said he was in that certain missionary frame of mind. He started to speak.

"Look out, Samuel," Patterson said, "here it comes."

"Even you two must admit that it is a glorious thing, what man can accomplish," he said. "When there is a common splendid goal, there are no limits. Think what will be done when we all have God's warmth in our hearts."

Samuel's eyes had closed; he began to snore. Patterson couldn't help laughing.

"I am immune to your disdain," Starling said, as good-natured as ever. He looked at them both closely. "When I came here, I had but one small goal: to convert the entire continent of Africa." He shook his head. "Now I've decided to move on to something *really* difficult: I will not rest until both of you are safely in the fold."

"I have had four wives," Samuel said. "Good luck."

"The struggle is the glory . . ." Starling said philosophically.

The three friends, for each of whom the struggle meant a different thing, smiled at each other.

TWENTY-FIVE

The train was departing the Tsavo station, heading back toward the coast. It passed a group of Hindus working on the line along the edge of a large grassy field, reballasting temporary roadbed with broken stone, converting it to permanent.

One of the men started a chant, which the others soon picked up. It was exceptionally pretty.

Down at the bridge site, Patterson waded into the river, but stopped as the sound of the chant came distantly to him on the wind.

He listened as the song grew louder. Were the Indians chanting louder, or was it the shifting wind? He gazed across the plain. It was turning into a stunner of a day—glorious blue sky broken up by pale clouds.

Then new voices. Another song, nearer to him on the right of way between the station and the bridge. There a bunch of African workers started a chant of their own, rather softly at first. *"Ooo loo sha sha, ooo loo sha sha . . ."*

Then they too started to sing louder.

It was becoming a lovely musical duel.

Starling, circling one of his thorn fortifications in

the Hindu area, paused briefly, listening to the sounds of the men. He took off his little sunglasses and rubbed the sweat from his eyes and beamed. It was a world of God's making.

On the edge of the grassy field, the Indian men worked and sang harder, as the coast train chuffed into the distance, trailing its anthracite smoke back over them.

The hot, shifting midday breeze fanned the grass behind the singing men, moving it back and forth. They paid heed only to their work, and to their pleasurable song.

Then something that was not grass moved, something low to the ground, inscribing a flicking half circle through the grass.

Patterson, down beside the bridge, walked in the water and listened to the sound of the men and the birds. The sun was high in the sky. The air was cool by the river under the swaying borassus trees.

The Indian men at the grassy field beyond the station started a new chant, answering the African crew.

Down in the grass, something moved again, only the other way this time, flicking back in another 180-degree arc.

Patterson waded out of the river onto the bank on the near side by a tree.

Out past the station, the wind vibrated the tall yellowing grasses behind the Indian workers. Their chant filled the air.

And here it came again, that shudder in the grass flicking in a different direction.

Patterson looked up at someone coming fast along the embankment above. It was Samuel, running down the tracks. He held an envelope in his hand as he ran toward the bridge.

Another movement stirred in the grassy field behind the Hindu workers beyond the station. A tail whipped into sight, quivering.

Samuel ran down the riverbank toward Patterson with the letter. "For you," he said, pushing it forward.

Patterson took it. "Thank you, Samuel," he said, turning the letter over.

Samuel watched as Patterson opened it. "Good news?" he said.

"I expect so," Patterson said, glancing at the letter. "It's from my wife."

"Do you like her?" Samuel said.

"I do, actually, very much," Patterson said.

Samuel flashed his wonderful smile. "Don't like any of mine," he said.

He walked away. Patterson smiled after him.

In the Hindu area, Starling was probing at the thorn fence around one of the outermost tent clusters, searching out any last weaknesses.

Behind him in the tall grass, the only sound was the gentle swishing of the foliage in the breeze. Then a ripple of color moving up, then stillness again.

TWENTY-SIX

Starling, intent on his work, noticed nothing except the sound of the singing men out past the station, singing their melodic chant.

Patterson, by the river, opened his letter.

There was a large tree up the riverbank, where the high yellowing grasses came down closest to the tracks. The tree cast a large shadow across the ground, and within the shadow, something moved, shifting in the dark. Or was there nothing?

Patterson, intent on his reading, noticed nothing. He heard Helena's voice as he read: *Darling, the big excitement yesterday was when some schoolchildren spotted a whale. They were looking at me, John.*

Patterson smiled. He saw in his mind's eye his wife, in their bedroom, moving across to the window staring out. She now had a considerable stomach.

That was an attempt at humor, he heard her say in his head as he read on. *But I don't feel very funny these days. I miss you terribly, and after our son—I still have total confidence that it will be a son—well, after he's born I think travel might be broadening. As he kicks me at night I'm quite sure he's telling me he definitely wants to come to Africa. Thought you might need reminding.*

Patterson, by the flowing water, smiled and folded the letter.

Somewhere in the grass then, not far back in the yellowing field just past the Tsavo station, was a thing never seen before. It was an animal tail, but this was stuck straight out, like a finger, like a road parallel to the ground. Not switching back and forth, but pointing, vibrating ever so slightly.

The singing workmen near the Tsavo station passed half-filled bushels of broken stone hand to hand down a long line of men. They really concentrated on their melody, making it sound even better. As the last bushel left the hands of the last man something stepped out of the tall grass unknown to anyone there—unknown to anyone anywhere for that matter. A white-maned lion stepped out of the tall grass. It was enormous. Heart-stopping. Easily five hundred pounds. It just stood there, in the open beyond the grassy field, tail stuck out straight behind it.

Then, without warning, it charged, racing faster than anything that size could move except in dreams.

The workers, about twenty of them, bolted in the other direction, running, screaming for their lives.

By the bridge, Patterson turned his head sharply.

At the Hindu stockade, Starling did the same.

At the work site the screaming workmen were scattering, running, shrieking past two yelling guards, one firing wildly, the other dropping his weapon. Both immediately joined the fleeing, panicked workers. Some of them just started to cry, running with all their might, knowing they would never outdistance the beast.

A fat worker puffing along the tracks toward the station glanced back. He realized he had run the wrong way!

What occurred next happened so fast it must have been like a bad dream for the fat worker, a horrible slow-motion phantasmagoria, a sick falling, a black wave of night enveloping him.

The gigantic white-maned lion leapt onto the fat worker, brought him to earth, and bit his neck nearly in two, snuffing his life out.

TWENTY-SEVEN

Patterson and Samuel raced up from the river.

Starling ran from the fenced Hindu sleeping camp toward the station, holding a rifle in his hands.

In the part of camp by the forge and the equipment warehouse, a bunch of workmen froze as the screams reached them. They fell back, startled, as Patterson rushed past on the way to his tent area, Samuel pounding after him.

Patterson raced to his tent, grabbing the same rifle that had killed the first lion, along with a shotgun and some cartridges.

Starling, running flat out, was heading toward the station.

Patterson charged along the railroad tracks, loading his rifle on the fly. He passed the shotgun to Samuel.

Samuel, carrying the ammunition, tried to load as he ran behind Patterson, all the while trying to keep up.

As they neared the railroad station, Starling joined up with them in a dead run. Patterson led the three of them around the building toward the work area.

They emerged in the work area, and nothing was

visible now. The workers were gone, and from this angle, it looked deserted.

They moved slowly toward the other side of the station, then they stopped.

They heard odd sounds from around the corner. Patterson glanced at Starling. The sounds could only have been the crunching of bones.

Patterson slowed, checking his rifle.

Starling did the same. Samuel, holding the extra ammunition, moved close to Patterson.

Patterson suddenly stepped away from the platform, rounding the corner, and just as he did, the white-maned lion and the fat worker came into view, the lion crouching, crunching at the fat worker's feet.

Patterson, with Starling now next to him, stared in horror.

The lion rose and circled around the body toward the station.

Patterson moved out into clearer view, Starling right with him. The lion was still a good distance away.

The lion, a low growl emerging from his throat, took the worker's body by the shoulder, and began backing away with it.

Samuel moved out from the corner behind the other two men.

Patterson dropped to his knees for the shot. Starling did the same. And as they both raised their rifles, the white lion growled louder and, moving fast, pulled the body deeper into the shadows at the far end of the station.

Patterson sighted down the barrel at the back of the beast, found his aim, and was about to fire when Samuel cried out and pointed back toward the roof of the station above them.

A black shadow was suddenly there, this monstrous dark thing that appeared from the flat-roofed part of the station and moved across the sun, actually blocking out its rays. Fully stretched out, it seemed to go on forever.

Patterson and Starling, turning simultaneously, saw the great length of the mysterious shape just as it launched itself.

The enormous black-maned lion dove into the three men, sending them sprawling. With a deafening roar, it was off running across the Tsavo station toward the white-maned lion. The white-maned lion, roaring in response, turned. And the two lions, one as eerie and pale as a ghost, the other as dark and foreboding as night, stood and looked back at the men.

The Ghost had blood and chunks of flesh on its mouth. And the Darkness had crazed eyes that pierced the very souls of the onlooking men.

They were bringers of destruction, these two. They were able to kill the old and the young and the fat and the strong—anyone and everyone who came across their path.

Patterson, lying in pain, dazed, his left shoulder bleeding, tried to reach for his rifle as the Ghost and the Darkness moved away slowly, almost insolently, toward the field of tall grass, roaring and gnashing their murderous fangs.

Samuel lay in shock.

Patterson reached the rifle, and as he managed to lift it and fire, the roaring sounds grew deafening. Patterson's gun was ready to fire again, but it was futile. The lions were far out of range now, and he knew it.

The two wild-maned males backed into the tall grass. They roared one final time, and then, they were gone. The grass was full of moving patterns from the wind, and that was all the men now saw. Just the grass blowing this way and that.

Patterson staggered to his feet, staring at the grassy field. "Jesus, two of them . . ." he said.

Samuel, dazed, struggled up and pointed.

Patterson suddenly registered Samuel's gesture. He turned and saw Starling, lying dead, his throat ripped open.

Samuel moved to Starling's side, speaking in a strained voice. *"Vipi wewe mdogo wangu? Nilikuambia uwe mwangalifu!"* he said. "What's wrong with you, little brother? I told you to be careful!"

TWENTY-EIGHT

The train from Mombasa was arriving. It would make the loop at the Tsavo station and head back.

A horde of Indian workmen—nearly a hundred men—stampeded up the hill toward the station, carrying their possessions with them. They ran like men desperate to escape the worst place on earth.

"You're the foreman, Abdullah," Patterson said in a raised voice. "Stop these men." He stood on the platform watching a sizable portion of his work force making ready to leave.

Abdullah shrugged in his arrogant way. "They are too frail to work. Be content I have decided to stay."

None of the Indian workmen streaming onto the platform looked remotely frail in appearance. They were chattering to each other in their native dialects, excited and thankful to be escaping with their lives.

Samuel stood in the shade of the platform with his wooden staff, looking grave, watching the argument intently.

Patterson gestured toward the hissing, steam-enveloped train, which was close to stopping now. "Beaumont is on that train," he said to Abdullah. "He sees this chaos, and you'll lose your job."

"So will you," Abdullah said insolently. "That's all you really care about."

"You think so? Fine," Patterson said, raising a hand to signal that he was finished arguing.

The defecting workmen were crowding down the platform, hoping to be first on the slowing train, desperate not to be left off.

"It's best you get out," Patterson said to Abdullah, his voice dripping contempt. "Go. Tell all your people to go, run home where they'll be safe under the covers, and when the bridge is built and the railroad is done, they can tell their women that out of all the thousands who worked here, they were the only ones to flee."

He wheeled around, and started to walk away.

Abdullah and the men, hearing Patterson's tone, listened to hurried translations from English-speaking workers. They went quiet, staring after Patterson.

Samuel cocked an eye, witnessing a change in the men's attitude. Just a small shift, but it was clear that Patterson had won. The two of them exchanged a quick glance and turned to the train to see Robert Beaumont appear in the door of a passenger car, formidable and handsome as ever.

Despite the very long journey from England, and the two-day journey up from Mombasa through the dust and the tropical heat and humidity, somehow the man's clothes were still crisp. He took off his white fedora as he surveyed the area. He wiped his brow, then his hands, with a white handkerchief. His white vested suit was quite free of the red dust of Tsavo.

Beaumont's two valets stood behind him with his personal cases and valises.

Patterson and Samuel moved up.

"Pleasant journey?" Patterson asked, as Beaumont stepped down with his infamous smile.

Beaumont cast a cool eye over his crack bridge builder. This unshaven, red-eyed fellow wearing a sweat-stained, open-collared bush outfit was not the same spit-and-polish model officer he had sent forth from his offices in London.

"How could it be a pleasant journey?" Beaumont said. "I hate Africa."

The sudden sound of men singing rose up behind them. Patterson looked around to behold a miracle of miracles. The men had started walking back down the hill. They were singing the same song that the workmen sang just before the Ghost and the Darkness attacked. It was pretty, but nonetheless, it was also a little unnerving.

Beaumont listened a moment. "Lovely sound," he said. "They seem happy."

"Don't they, though?" Patterson said.

"So work must be going well?" Beaumont said.

Patterson looked up and down the platform. "Where are the soldiers?" he asked. "I asked for reinforcements."

"I told you that you were on your own," Beaumont said coldly. "There will be no soldiers here."

"The men need protection," Patterson said.

Abdullah passed by, bowing slightly and waving conspicuously. "Morning, friend," he piped to Patterson, "glorious day."

Patterson gave him a jaundiced look. "Yes, yes, aren't they all," he said.

Abdullah moved off with a self-satisfied smirk.

"Where is Starling?" Beaumont asked, looking around. "A while back he ordered some Bibles." He indicated a crate that porters were putting down nearby. "I've brought them. Is he here?"

Samuel tilted his head. "Here he comes now," he said quietly.

Beaumont turned to see half a dozen natives carrying Starling's coffin, trudging up the rise and stepping up onto the platform. They stopped at an open boxcar and started to load the coffin onto the train.

Beaumont watched, stunned. He turned and glared furiously at Patterson, his face turning red in anger.

TWENTY-NINE

Patterson, Samuel, and Hawthorne stood quietly as Beaumont surveyed the scene in the hospital.

It was far more crowded than the last time. Every cot was filled, and there were workers lying on pallets on the floor. It was still under control, but barely so.

A few of these patients were actual casualties of the lion, clawed or otherwise injured in the frantic run to escape. The rest were emotional casualties: basket cases of raw fear and malingerers feigning malaria or some disabling suffering of gut or limb.

Beaumont stalked the length of the gloomy tent. His reaction could hardly have been more icy. He gestured sharply toward Hawthorne to join them, and spoke low and fast to his three employees.

"What in hell is going on?" he said.

"The Ghost and the Darkness have come," Samuel said.

"In English," Beaumont snapped.

"It's what the natives are now calling the lions," Patterson said. "Two lions have been causing trouble."

"So what?" Beaumont said. "This is Africa. And I thought you were a hunter."

"It hasn't been that simple so far," Patterson said.

Beaumont couldn't believe what he was hearing. "How many have they killed?" he asked.

Patterson nodded for the doctor to answer.

Hawthorne had no use for this rich exploiter and his dictatorial ways. Plus he had been drinking. He hated the idea of men dying for a self-serving ignoramus like this.

He took his time, under the guise of absolute accuracy, in coming to an answer. "Well, of course, I can't supply a totally accurate figure," Hawthorne said, "because there are those that are actually authenticated and there are those that we once thought were workers killing each other or deserting from camp, so any number I give is subject to error—"

"*How many?*" Beaumont barked, tired of Hawthorne's droning.

Patterson answered bluntly. "Thirty, I should think."

"Christ!" Beaumont said, jolted, looking from man to man.

Sour-faced, sweating in the blistering afternoon sun, Beaumont looked up from the plans to the bridge, down at the plans again and at the timeline inscribed on them, then back at the bridge.

Patterson and Samuel, with him on the embankment, suffered this examination in silence.

Little substantial work had been accomplished since the man-eaters began their direct assault on the Tsavo camp, where the taking of Mahina had occurred. Just a few men climbed on the bridge structure now, working slowly. And now there were guards with rifles patrolling it.

Beaumont slammed the plans down and shot Patterson a deadly look. "You've been here three months and you are already behind schedule," he said with scorn. "Don't you know the Germans and the French are right behind you? I don't care about your problems and I don't care about the thirty dead. I care about my knighthood, and if this railroad finishes on schedule, I'll get my knighthood and *I want it.*" He saved his sharpest sarcasm for Patterson. *"What are you planning to do?"*

Patterson met the man's gaze. He was a doer, not an arguer. He turned away sharply and walked off, headed for the inner camp and the equipment warehouse.

THIRTY

It was something very odd, even for the anything-goes wilds of Africa.

A small railroad boxcar sat in a copse of bleached thorn trees far off the narrow-gauge tracks. It was nowhere near the station; rather, it was far into the bush, positioned right on a game trail, and near the place the white-maned lion had taken Mahina's body to eat.

It had taken thirty men to roll it and drag it to this deserted area. In fact, half that many workers could have done it. None would consent to venturing so far into the bush, however, unless many went together, along with guards with repeating rifles watching on every side.

Several workers were wrestling a green army tent up and over the boxcar, trying to disguise the fact that the small railroad car was, indeed, nothing but a small railroad car.

It was unwieldy work and the men were perspiring heavily, all the while watching the bush for any movement.

"I'm calling it my 'contraption,'" Patterson said, as

he and Beaumont approached. "We're going to surround it with a boma—a fence to you—and we're going to leave a small opening opposite that door."

"This is supposed to be salvation?" Beaumont said, staring at the contraption. "What kind of lunacy are we dealing with here?"

Patterson gestured for Beaumont to follow him inside the railroad car through the open door at one end.

They clambered into the empty, echoing car. Beaumont looked around at the shadowed space. Sunlight stabbed through the horizontal slats of the boxcar walls and striped the floor. He shook his head skeptically.

The car had been divided in half by thick metal bars from floor to ceiling. The bars were close together, with only a few inches between them.

"In that half will be bait," Patterson said, pointing through the bars to the other end. "Human bait. I'll start things off." He pointed to the open doorway. "A sliding door will fit above that and a tripwire will run across the floor."

Beaumont's ambiguously charming smile was back. "Genius," he said. "The beast will enter, tripping the wire, and the door will slide down, trapping him. You, safe behind the bars, will have him at your mercy and will shoot him."

Patterson nodded.

Beaumont exploded. "Are you running a high fever, man?" he said. "How could you conceive of something so idiotic?"

"I didn't conceive of it for the lions," Patterson said.

"I built one in India when there was trouble with a tiger."

"And it *worked?*" Beaumont said, incredulous.

"In point of fact, it didn't," Patterson said, hating to admit it. Yet he pressed on, undeterred. "But I'm convinced the theory is sound."

Beaumont snorted in response.

The two men moved outside. Patterson knocked the slats of the boxcar, preoccupied with the sturdiness of his trap and the soundness of his plan. He was aware of Beaumont watching him with clear disdain. The tension and ill will the man could generate was almost unbearable.

Beaumont looked at Patterson for a long moment, then said at last, "I made a mistake hiring you. I wanted someone with intelligence. The world is watching us. I'm not bringing troops here. Why didn't you hire a professional hunter? I'm going to locate Remington. I assume you've heard of him."

Patterson was unfazed. "Every man who's ever hunted has heard of him," he said evenly. "I wish he were here right now. And I hope by the time you find him, the lions will be dead and I'll be back on schedule."

Beaumont said nothing, just stared at Patterson.

"What?" Patterson said after a moment or two of silence.

"Just deciding your future, Patterson," he said. "And for now the job is still yours—only because it would take me so long to find a replacement, certainly not because of any quality you've demonstrated so far. I'm going up the line to check the surveying teams.

By the time I return, if I have to take any further action myself, you're finished."

He walked a half circle around Patterson, eyeing him contemptuously, letting his words sink in. "And I promise I will do everything within my considerable power to destroy your reputation," he said. "Fair enough?" He flashed the great smile. "Told you you'd hate me." He turned and walked off.

Samuel, carrying a burlap bag, moved up to Patterson as soon as Beaumont was out of earshot.

"I do hate him," Patterson said, staring after Beaumont. He took the bag from Samuel, opened it, and pulled out flares.

"I want you to distribute one bag of rocket flares to every tent area," he said. "Tell the men not to set them off unless there's an attack."

He returned to his trap, helping the men pull scrub undergrowth around the wheels to hide them.

THIRTY-ONE

Flickering shadows rippled the walls of the converted boxcar. Patterson, bleary with fatigue, sat in a corner of the car, writing a letter by the light of a hurricane lantern turned low.

Helena, he wrote. *It's gotten very strange here. None of this started until I arrived, and I feel it's entirely up to me to stop it. And I won't give up until I do. But these lions—and it's probably my imagination—but they don't behave as lions always have. The bridge is falling farther behind schedule, and since Starling's death, I feel even Samuel is losing faith in me.*

He paused and read over what he had written. Then he scrunched the paper up into a little ball and took another sheet.

Dearest, he wrote. *It is so beautiful here. Peace and tranquillity continue to abound. The workers report each day with a smile. I am rested and happy and find myself singing when I least expect it. Your John.*

Suddenly, through the open door at the far end,

the arc of a flare rising over the distant camp cut the night sky.

Patterson jumped as though jabbed with a spear. He watched the flare fall back out of sight beyond the thorn-tree forest. He closed his eyes and prayed not to hear screams in the distance, sinking into misery.

Patterson departed his trap emptyhanded in the morning. He made his way back to the Tsavo camp to take inventory, hoping the night had been quiet.

The boma around one of the Indian areas was destroyed. He stood with Hawthorne and watched stretchers being carried out. Dead were lying inside. Patterson now knew for sure: These were not ordinary lions.

Patterson knew lion habits. They were lazy animals. The big male would lie around and let the females go in packs at night and make the kills. Only then would the males finally bestir themselves, trot out to the kill, push in and eat their fill.

After a big kill, when their stomachs were full, they would lie around, resting and sleeping twenty hours a day or more until they were hungry again.

These big males, by contrast, were out marauding and killing, for themselves, almost night after night. They were not killing just to eat. And they were ignoring all other prey.

The two had developed a taste for a slow-moving, easy-to-hunt, easy to find prey. A prey that had gathered all its members together in one relatively confined area of a few square miles, the same area by the river night after night.

It was a lion's buffet.

The renegades had accustomed themselves to the joy of warm, salty human blood in their mouths at every opportunity.

Which was far from standard lion behavior.

The African workers had their own theories on how it came to be. These two enraged beasts, the Ghost and the Darkness, were *shaitaini,* they said. Devils of the night. The *shaitaini* were punishing the intruders for the deaths of certain tribal chiefs months before. Another version held that the famine that had struck the tribes along the Athi River also put the squeeze on the lions, driving them to alternative foods.

Whichever it was, the white intruders had brought it on themselves, of that they were certain.

Patterson secretly suspected the latter theory was true. The railroad game takers had driven the local herds afar. The indolent lions had been wildly successful in slaking their new taste for human flesh; why travel farther?

But how had they developed this new taste? Patterson suspected he knew the answer to that too, but it was a matter of some delicacy.

He had learned that there had been a spate of deaths by fever among Indians working on the permanent way back along the rail line, many miles out from the base camp. When a death occurred out there, the workers, unable to provide proper ritual cremations, sometimes gave their deceased colleagues symbolic cremations by leaving their wrapped bodies lying in the bush along the line with live coals in their mouths.

Lions from miles away no doubt picked up the scent and came padding through the darkness to investigate. They ravenously fell upon the corpses. Some of them soon developed a strong liking for human flesh. Two of them, in particular, were stalking just outside Tsavo camp. . . .

THIRTY-TWO

The bridge, in the dead of night, was now as occupied as during the day. Some Indian workmen huddled, high over the water, on the partial span that had been completed. They had rifles, and had begun to spend nights there for protection, taking turns sleeping.

They were not sleeping well. These lions seemed uncanny in their abilities. If they wanted to swim the muddy Tsavo and climb the piers, they probably could. Still, the bridge sitters assured themselves, the other men up in the camp would surely be easier meals, wouldn't they?

Up in the camp, the trees were full. They were populated by men who had contrived ways to sleep high off the ground. Some even sought shelter under the ground: sleeping in stifling graves they had dug in the earth and covered with heavy timbers. Some slept inside hot, cramped, galvanized water tanks.

Nowhere felt completely safe from the two phantoms who were now striking with ruthless regularity.

During the day these same men—not so many men as before, but still a valuable number—worked diligently on the bridge, driven a little by pride, but more for the promise of bonuses of many rupees. They were making a calculated gamble with their lives for a shinier future back across the Indian Ocean.

But now progress was maddeningly slow.

It was just past midday. Patterson was not at his usual post overseeing work at the bridge.

Samuel was there, however, talking with Abdullah. They both turned suddenly at the sound of gunfire.

The multiple cracks echoed away—bad news again, no doubt. They turned earnestly back to each other, hoping to quickly resolve the problem of the moment. Indeed, they were hoping to get on with finishing this bridge quickly and escaping this nightmarish workplace.

Out in the belt of bushland, more gunfire sounded.

In the thorn-tree fence around the railroad car, a tree branch with claw thorns and numerous red flowers trembled in the wall of the boma.

"Fire!" Patterson commanded again.

Multiple rifle shots. The branch was destroyed, the flowers exploded in a burst of color.

Patterson stood behind the riflemen—three Indian workers—just beyond his boxcar contraption. The workers looked like brothers, which they were. They also looked tough, which they were as well. They were three Pathan street fighters, Afghanis from the north of India.

Patterson walked up and examined their shooting. He was impressed. "Very good indeed," he said.

The middle worker bowed his head slightly and said with a twisted smile. "We have hunted since childhood." He gave a casual shrug.

"All right," Patterson said with genuine enthusiasm. "You'll spend your nights inside." He nodded toward the railroad car. They bobbed their heads in return. "You'll have plenty of ammunition. You're totally protected, you really have nothing to fear."

"That is correct," the middle worker said. He looked at his brothers. "Nothing."

Patterson looked at the three swaggering young men. Immortal, each of them. Obviously, he could not have chosen better.

THIRTY-THREE

The three brothers sat in the railroad car muttering to each other in their clucking Pathan tongue. They were tough as ever, secure behind the iron bars, fearless. Only a dim light shone in the boxcar, gleaming off the barrels of their guns. They were ready for anything.

But nothing was happening. Silence. The human bait fingered their triggers, leaned against the end wall, and watched the open door at the other end.

They had no doubt that the lions would come and glory would be theirs. This was cherrypicking. Luck was theirs to have been selected for such a simple chore.

Thick ground mist had crept up from the river over the Tsavo camp. One eerie red light slid swiftly through the miasma from one side of the camp to the other—a hurricane lantern in the hands of a native guard late to get to the water tower, which had been converted into a fortified gun tower.

At the bridge site, the river palms clicked in the

light breeze. Black water flowed steadily past the palms and the bridge piers.

Upstream from the piers, dozens of workers, terrified of the foggy darkness ashore, waded right into the river for safety. They waded out until the water came up to their necks. They reached out, held hands, and started to sing.

Above them, the finished portion of the bridge was now crowded with men seeking safety. They slept in snatches, waking at any movement. When the singing started below, many on the bridge sang along softly with them.

Samuel, standing erect with his staff on the water tower by the station, cast a cold eye across the misty landscape. He knew there was very little chance the lions would simply move on to another killing ground. He knew they wouldn't wander away until they had killed every last living morsel in Tsavo. Or were slain first.

He saw a flare somewhere in the outer circle of tents. He prayed for the crack of gunshots. Please . . .

No gunshots sounded. But a flurry of screams soon echoed from far off. The guards on the tower all stared out at the dying flare, dumb with terror.

Patterson moved to a better vantage point in his tree-hide. He had stationed himself above Mahina's tent again, hoping the lions would return.

He listened to the lovely sound of the men singing down at the river. Then he saw a flare rise and listened helplessly for the next sound. Faint screams reached his ears and obliterated the singing.

He looked in the direction of the camp and could just make out, between himself and the shape of the water tower, silhouetted workers in trees and on corrugated iron roofs of equipment and supply sheds—for the moment, beyond the merciless claws.

THIRTY-FOUR

A shimmering sun fell upon the grassy plain. Three miles out from Tsavo, the two lions walked through the long grass on a converging path with a herd of Thomson's gazelles.

Upwind of the lions, the tiny, dainty-footed gazelles moved along a well-worn trail toward a water source. The wind shifted, and the gazelles suddenly smelled lion. They scattered, bounding and twisting in all directions, unsure where the danger lay.

One young gazelle made exactly the wrong choice. Dashing straight at the lions concealed by the grass, it saw the beasts much too late. It couldn't change direction, so it sprang high to go over them. The white-maned lion, with honed reflexes, reached up a huge paw and knocked the miniature gazelle out of the air. The little animal hit the ground and didn't move, its back broken.

The lions barely looked at it and continued on their stealthy march through the grass.

Yes, the gazelle was prey. In lean times, a succulent tidbit worth fighting over. But now it was not even an hors-d'oeuvre; an unwanted diversion for two giants with ravening appetites.

The object of their straight-ahead march came into view on the far side of the water hole.

A dozen longhorn cattle held in a makeshift *kraal*. Cattle were highly valued among the tribes as food, currency, or even for barter. Two Swahili herdsmen armed with spears guarded them alertly.

The cattle were nervous. One of them kicked anxiously at the wind. And they had every reason to be nervous.

The Ghost and the Darkness casually stepped out of the tall grass and ambled straight toward the herdsmen.

The men spun, saw the two monsters, and hurled their spears wildly. They took off at a terrified run for the biggest tree on the edge of the closest *kopje* and climbed it.

The Ghost stepped through the rail fence and walked among the cattle. The longhorns squealed and kicked in fear. The Ghost chose one to kill, leapt on it, and brought it to earth with its meat-hook claws imbedded in its back. The cow screamed. The dust rose around the lion as it scrambled to the head of the downed animal and clamped its huge jaws on its muzzle. Within moments the paralyzed creature had suffocated. The Darkness ambled over to join in the feast.

Patterson, in another tree-hide on another night, sat alone with his hunting rifle. The futile nights and losing battles had left him with sunken, yellowed eyes in a scowling, unquiet face.

An owl alighted in the tree above him. It sat on a high swaying branch and ratcheted its head this way and that, on the lookout. It saw nothing and was silent.

The next day was no easier. Patterson had to lead the handful of available workers almost by force to the bridge worksite.

There was much tension in the air. Abdullah and his men hardly worked. Abdullah would walk past Patterson, look at him, and without even nodding, look away. Things were clearly about to explode.

In frustration, Patterson picked up an abandoned tool and went vigorously to work on the bridge. But his fervent labor changed nothing.

Patterson patroled at night with his hunting gun, making rounds of the inner and outer tents, the hospital, the supply buildings, the bridge site, the thorn bomas. He skirted the outer darkness, inviting the beasts to try him. He flicked a lantern beam over the high grass, looking for the gleam of eyes like yellow quartz.

He sat for many nights in different trees around the outer circle of the thorn-fenced tents, during different kinds of weather. He would check his rifle, put a blanket around his back, and wait in utter, unmoving silence.

Some nights, he and the whole camp would hear the faraway, hollow sound of a lion call, then the terrifying silence as the stalking commenced. At such times, in uncontrollable fear, the men would scream and fire their rifles and bang on their mess tins.

It did no good. The killings went on.

But never where Patterson sat, always elsewhere.

Two Punjabis disappeared from near their tent

where they had gone to relieve themselves in a night monsoon. The next day, the drag marks led the searchers on almost a straight line to the feast scenes.

One body was found three hundred yards upriver, three-quarters eaten. The other workman was found on his back on the riverbank nearby, a stork standing on his chest, eating his eyes.

An African messenger returning with a letter in a cleft stick from Charles Beaumont near Lake Victoria got as far as the hippo path beyond the outer circle of tents. There he had climbed a tree, and a lion had chewed off his leg and lapped the falling arterial blood until there was no more to drink.

The message for which the man died was eventually delivered to Patterson. It was little more than a rhapsodic travelogue, hardly worth a man's life.

Over a short period of weeks, four *jemadars* disappeared. When three of them were found with their throats torn open, limbs clawed and slashed but bodies *un*eaten, there was suspicion that they had been murdered for profit by rival clansmen or their own coolies, since headmen always carried money. None of the bodies was found with any money in the pockets.

But most of the disappearances—discounting the steady stream of desertions—were because of the lions, and unmistakably so.

Late one sweltering night, blood-chilling screams at a well-constructed boma brought Patterson running. He found the thorn fence tunneled out, with shreds of lion fleece hanging on the thorns. Inside, two Indians were viciously clawed. A third was found the next day, just a tooth-punctured, turbaned head and discarded rib cage.

Patterson's face, as he failed during the day to build, and then again and again at night to make a kill, underwent a terrible change. Joy in eyes that had once looked upon the blood-colored volcanic outcroppings of Tsavo as mere foundation for accomplishment had turned to hooded stares of guilt.

Man was the intruder here, not the lions, of that much he was certain. If the bridge were suddenly finished, and the human settlement pulled up and dispersed, the lions would not then range far and wide for human flesh. Overnight they would settle down and return to their lethargic, zebra-hunting ways.

The excessive human encroachment was at fault. It was a male lion's second most important job, next to procreating, to provide a secure territory for his pride's lionesses to have cubs. This pullulating ant colony of humans was fouling his domain. He was genetically loaded to respond.

But Patterson also was following the dictates of his nature. He would not run from a fight; rather, he would charge into the jaws of it, and keep charging from every angle he could find.

Something had to happen, and it soon did.

THIRTY-FIVE

Something was rustling around in the other end of the railroad car.

The three workers, the fearless brothers, lounged in the closed end of the contraption, two of them asleep, a flickering lamp the only illumination in the car.

For a moment the one awake brother didn't know what it was. Nothing more than a change in the texture of blackness in the open door of the car. He stared hard, hoping it was what he was waiting for.

The tripwire gleamed in the faint light.

And then, suddenly, a paw walked across it, and the instant that happened the door of the railroad car slammed down loudly and the Pathan gunman pushed himself to his feet and gaped. There it loomed.

The Darkness, standing alone in one half of the railroad car.

It was incredible, but Patterson's idea had actually worked. The boxcar, with the thick bars separating the two halves, had caught its prey. In one half, the huge lion stood staring at the three armed, tough workers in the other side.

For a moment, it could have been a frozen tableau,

as both sides were too startled and surprised to do anything but stare.

And then all hell just *exploded.*

The Darkness erupted, a thunderous roar coming from his throat, the kind of ground-shaking bellow that could be heard five miles away in the night. But in the enclosed room, it was just overwhelming, incapacitating. And then it got much worse.

The man-eater threw its massive body at the bars, both front legs flailing through, slashing at the three tough workers with hooked, bladed claws. The three men, hearts pounding in their throats, slammed back against the rear wall of the car.

The Darkness backed off a step, rumbling.

The workers, the mettle drained from their hard faces, froze against the rear wall, unable to do anything but quake in fright.

With another immense roar, the lion launched himself forward again, claws up, ripping at the air, smashing into the bars.

The men looked up in horror at the ceiling where the bars were connected. The sheer power of the leap had made them jiggle just the least bit.

The Darkness came again, howling as his body hit the bars. Fully ten feet long, five hundred pounds of killer hit the iron grid. The ceiling and the bars shook, but they were not giving way.

The tough workers began to realize this. And one of them, through the raging and roaring and shaking of the iron and the giant claws raking at them, gathered himself enough to raise his long gun and try to draw a bead.

The second worker jerked his gun up too. And then the third brother was ready and all three fired.

The quarter-ton monster never flinched, never backed off an inch. He roared even more, and slammed the bars repeatedly, loosening them a little more at the top.

The brothers reloaded and fired again.

And reloaded again.

One of the workers noticed blood splashing on his arm and he gaped at the lion and saw no wound. He spun around and then slapped at his own head, looking for the source of the blood. And he found it: It was coming out of his ears!

He tried to twist away from the blood from his own ears and kicked over the lamp, igniting a fire.

Flames crawled up one slatted wall, and it began to look like hell in there.

The man-eater at the bars *stood up* and seemed to fill the car, towering over everything. It was a hideous nightmare, a demon from hell come to kill them.

The workers staring up at the giant being were more terrified than they ever thought possible, paralyzed with fear. The Darkness towered, pounding the bars, roaring horribly as the flames brightened, licking up one side of the slatted boxcar.

The tough men moved away from the flames, palsied with the deafening roars of the beast, and fired again. The Darkness was going crazy on his side of the car, slashing, leaping, and slamming against the bars, which were somehow barely holding.

The workers reloaded in a frenzy, and the Darkness raced around the enclosed area, the flames rendering him Satanic—eyes of fire-yellow quartz, howls from the echoing abyss.

The three workers, firing again and reloading, firing again, reloading again, were beginning to realize that, amazing as it might seem, impossible as it might be to conceive, they were *missing*.

Sure, they were so goddamned scared and the Darkness was whirling on all sides, hitting the slats and bars and doors, roaring and leaping, but were they missing every single time?

They were hitting something—the thick wooden bars that slid down and held the door in place. Now, as the lion bashed the door, the workers started to hear the wooden bars beginning to splinter. And the Darkness, hearing this, whirled and leapt at the door. As they fired again, the bars gave, the door flopped open, and just like that, the man-eater was through it and gone.

The workmen sank to the floor of the boxcar and stared at the blackness of the open door.

The fire died out as though it too was exhausted.

The tough gunmen did not dare venture out into the feverish night.

THIRTY-SIX

It was just after dawn when Patterson stepped into the damaged, charred railroad car.

He stood where the Darkness had stood. The three workers were where they had spent the night, on the other side of the bars.

They told the story, quietly, over and over. All the details, every single shot. In subdued, chagrined, dumbfounded voices, they related the chronicle of their failure.

This was the most frustrating point yet for Patterson. Not only had his notion come so close to working only to fail, he could not comprehend how the workers had missed. It didn't seem possible.

"Not once?" he said several times. "You didn't hit it once?"

"I would never make excuses," the middle worker said, awe and fear in his voice. "But a fire broke out—the light was bad—he kept moving . . ."

"Well of course he kept moving," Patterson said. "But he couldn't have been more than ten feet away from the three of you. Surely you must have wounded the thing."

"I assure you we came close many times."

Samuel came from a tour of the boma. He pointed to the opening leading to and from the boxcar. "The pugs go there. There is no trace of blood anywhere."

Abdullah appeared in the opening in the fence. He approached the boxcar, followed by several dozen men. From Abdullah's face, Patterson could tell there was going to be a battle. His men were muttering and rumbling, backing him up.

"The next time we will do better," the middle worker said in a loud voice. His bravado wasn't convincing, even to himself.

Patterson made no reaction. He moved outside to meet the angry Indian headman.

Abdullah, simmering, moved straight to Patterson as he stepped down from the car. "The next time will be as this time," he said. "The Devil has come to Tsavo!"

Patterson was in no mood for this. "That's ridiculous talk, and you can't seriously believe it," he said.

Abdullah moved in closer. An undercurrent of anger ran through the tense crowd behind him as Patterson's words were translated and relayed. People were picking up rocks, pushing forward.

Abdullah rose up to his full height. "Now you're telling me my beliefs? I don't think so," he said.

"I wasn't and you know it, and don't push it," Patterson said flatly. "Listen, we have a problem in Tsavo—"

Abdullah cut in: "At last you're right. We do. *You* are the problem in Tsavo."

"Careful, Abdullah," Patterson said.

Patterson and Abdullah glared eye to eye. Behind

Abdullah, brown-faced turbaned men with cutlasses moved in closer.

The native revolts in Ethiopia and the Sudan, and the Wakamba slaughter of railroad workers on his own Uganda Line flashed through Patterson's mind. He looked across at the fearful, belligerent faces. He was greatly outnumbered. And, more important at that moment, he was unarmed.

Abdullah stepped toward him. "You do not tell me 'careful.' You do not tell me anything. You listen while I talk."

Patterson weighed his few options rapidly. Backing down was absolutely not one of them. The Uganda Line hung in the balance. His whole work force would break and run if Abdullah steamrollered him and walked away—or killed him. If he then somehow got out of this alive, it would take weeks, even months, to recruit and import more workers.

Which was exactly what the Germans and French were waiting for.

One major stumble and support for the British line would crumble. The Germans and French would push their alternate rail lines forward.

It would all be on Patterson's head. The man who couldn't manage a work force and build a simple bridge. The good name he had inherited from his father would be destroyed. It was fortunate, after all, that his father was gone and could not witness this debacle.

Patterson couldn't believe it had come to this.

He could think of no more words that would persuade. What was left of his authority was draining away by the second. He was without resource.

Then a shadow seemed to cross the space to Abdullah's left. Abdullah's eyes widened.

An enormous, double-barreled pistol was pressed hard against Abdullah's left temple.

A man's raspy voice growled, "Change in plan: You listen while *I* talk—because you have a question that needs answering. *Will I pull the trigger?*"

It was an American voice, with a rough Southern accent.

Remington had arrived.

He was one of those legends, ageless and powerful. A hardened professional hunter of reknowned skills who had seen everything and was capable of anything.

By looks, just a desperado. Rakish bush hat, unkempt hair to his shoulders, unshaven stubble. Rough-cut leather jacket criss-crossed by a bristling cartridge bandolier, knee-high cavalry boots. And an incredible swagger.

He seemed supremely capable of killing Abdullah. Very calmly, he cocked the pistol.

"He will pull the trigger, Abdullah," Samuel said matter-of-factly. "He'll kill you."

Without looking around to identify the speaker, Remington said, "No hints, Samuel."

"You don't know all that has happened here," Abdullah said without moving his head. "The Devil has come to Tsavo."

"You're right," Remington roared. "The Devil *has* come. Look at me! I am the Devil!"

Abdullah turned his head and stared at the twisted, smiling face of Remington. Yes, that man could easily have been the Devil, Abdullah thought.

Abdullah's whole demeanor changed. "I am a man of peace," he said, dripping conciliation.

"Am I to take it you want to live?" Remington said, spitting sarcasm.

"Most certainly," Abdullah said. "Absolutely. Yes."

"Excellent decision," Remington said. Then he suddenly reached out and shook Abdullah's hand. "Your name is Abdullah? I'm sure we'll meet again. Go and enjoy the splendid morning." He clapped the bug-eyed *jemadar* on the back.

"I think it's been a pleasure," Abdullah said, dazed. And with a slight nod of the head, he retreated. The ranks of the workers parted, and Abdullah disappeared among them.

He could be heard barking harsh commands. The throng instantly came apart and drifted away past the boma.

Remington turned and did another surprising thing: He embraced Samuel.

Remington pulled back and looked at Samuel. "You got old." He released the African and gestured toward the bush. "I'll stay with them," he said.

Fifty Masai warriors appeared over a rise and moved toward them out of the bush. They were big, powerful men, carrying spears, shields, and drums. They clearly did not take shit from anybody.

As the Masai approached, Remington and Samuel jabbered in Swahili.

"Umerudi," Samuel said. "You have returned."

"Rafiki yangu. Habari za siku nyingi?" Remington said. "My friend. How have you been these many days?"

"Sijambo," Samuel said. "I am well."

124

Remington turned and greeted his crew. *"Warani!"* he shouted. "Warriors!"

The Masai responded with a war cry.

Remington turned back to Samuel. *"Nitahitajl, Ng'ombe Kumi,"* he said. "I will need ten cows."

Remington turned to Patterson and looked him up and down. "I'm sure you're John Patterson," he said. And before Patterson could reply, he added, "Stay out of my way."

And without a word he was gone.

Patterson was left standing at the edge of the bush with Samuel. He stared at the Masai, with their long spears and decorated oval shields.

"Remington uses Masai when he hunts lions," Samuel explained. "It will cost us ten head of cattle."

Patterson continued to stare, digesting this new development.

"He takes some getting used to," Samuel said, reading Patterson's mind.

At that moment, Patterson would have given many hundred head of cattle for what Remington had just pulled off.

THIRTY-SEVEN

Remington walked around the crowded hospital tent, knocking his bush hat against his leg, his eyes flicking about, seeing everything, recognizing everything. Workers with dysentery, heat exhaustion, African tick fever, veldt sores; a man segregated at one end with suspected smallpox and other men on palliasses with fevers that had no names or known origins; a Punjabi dying of liver abscess; several workers with knife wounds, and the two workers who were clawed by the lions and had lived to have continuous nightmares about it.

He stopped by the lion victims and peeked under their dressings, examining the spread of the claw marks.

Someone lifted the tent flap and came in out of the glaring sunlight. It was Patterson, who took his hat off and looked around. Spotting Remington, he approached him. "I didn't have a chance to thank you," he said.

"What did I do?" Remington said, preoccupied.

"Got me out of trouble," Patterson answered.

Remington gave a matter-of-fact shrug. "Nonsense," he said. "Samuel would have done something. What was all that about?"

"Forty are dead," Patterson said.

"Extraordinary!" Remington said, excited.

"There's something you ought to know about these lions," Patterson started to say.

Remington cut in. "Let me save time," he said. "One, you are the engineer. Two, you are in charge of the bridge. Right so far?"

Patterson nodded.

"Good," Remington said. "Because, one, I am not an engineer. Two, I don't want to be in charge of the bridge. I'm sure you hate Tsavo as much as I do. And knowing Beaumont, you're not the imbecile he says you are, so let's help each other. I will help you by killing the lions and leaving, and you will help me by doing what I tell you so I can leave. See any problems?"

"Actually, no," Patterson said.

"All right," Remington said. "Let's prepare for battle." He suddenly took Patterson's hand and shook it. Then he turned away and continued his tour of the hospital.

Patterson walked along with him, unsure whether this was part of preparing for the battle. He looked around and quickly realized the hospital was even worse than when he last visited just a few days before. Bodies were crammed everywhere, and the sound of pain and sickness was constant.

"Before we do anything else," Remington said, "I propose we move the hospital." He grabbed the arm of Dr. Hawthorne as he hurried toward a screaming patient. "Build a new one by tomorrow night," he said peremptorily and started to move on.

"That's a terrible idea," Hawthorne stated flatly.

"Is it? I'm sorry," Remington said, appearing to backtrack. "But then of course you're the doctor, you should know."

"Most infantile notion I ever heard," Hawthorne said. "Why on earth should we go through all that?"

"I suppose I could answer you," Remington said, in a most charming manner now. "I suppose I could explain that the place is so inviting, what with the smell of blood and flesh, that they have to strike. It's even possible that I tell you I found some fresh paw marks around back, which means they're already contemplating feasting here."

He turned on Hawthorne then, his voice building. "But I don't want to answer you, because when you question me you are really saying that I don't have the least idea what I am doing. That I am nothing but an incompetent, that I am a fool." He turned to address the whole tent. "Anyone who finds me a fool, *please say so now.*"

Hawthorne's face quivered in fury, but he was terrified of this Cro-Magnon. He kept his peace.

Remington put on a nice smile. "Then we agree," he said. He turned and walked out.

THIRTY-EIGHT

Hawthorne sweated in the dispensary, supervising workers loading huge baskets with medical supplies and carrying them off.

A pile of bloody bandages was thrown out the flap. A stretcher was carried out by two workers, a groaning patient lying on top. The stretcher bearers turned left and marched up the rise.

Two other workers, their faces shielded in masks, dragged out the palliasse with the smallpox patient, who had died. They hurriedly wrapped the sheets around the body and turned right with it, down the hill toward the cremation site out beyond the thorn hedges.

The patient with dysentery was brought out, terribly swollen, his bowels ready to burst.

Patients with only scurvy and bush ulcers hobbled out of the old tent and up the hill on their own.

And as they hurried along—the patients and the bearers, the gun guards, the equipment and supply carriers—they looked around warily all the time, examining every tent shadow, flinching at every tree branch moving in the wind.

Every man in Tsavo acted that way now, in fear: of the lions, of disease, of the African tribes, of each other.

The labor truce brought about by Remington's fierce intervention was tenuous, vulnerable to the next lion onslaught.

Many workers simply absented themselves from work on the bridge to spend the day building boma and replenishing the huge piles of firewood for the night.

It was clear that Patterson could not protect them. Nor could this Remington, in all likelihood. Didn't these Englishmen understand? Primal forces were at work, gathering themselves like predators for the strike. Mere men couldn't hope to control them.

In daytime at the river, Patterson, exhausted and gray from many nights without sleep, watched his bridge progress not in feet but in inches.

He knew he would be the object of Beaumont's ridicule—the splendid Lt. Col. Patterson spending his nights perched in trees and blinds. Getting drubbed in a head-to-head conflict with two dumb brutes.

He couldn't backtrack. There was no place to go back to. He had to follow the impulsive Remington in his march forward, wither it led.

At Patterson's tent area, Samuel was organizing the removal of Patterson's tent and that of the camp's half-dozen orderlies. He instructed the workers to set it up near the African village area, farther from the bush.

Remington sat near the new hospital, in the shade

of a leafy borassus. He was eating sumptuously and watching the workers sweat.

The moving of the hospital had been a huge effort, and half of it had been completed the day before, despite the ever-present threat of murderous attack.

Orderlies carried the stretchers of wounded patients into the new hospital. It was on higher ground, constructed of fresh canvas and ringed by a tall boma. Samuel and Abdullah coordinated the action.

Hawthorne labored inside the new main tent, directing workers, unpacking, and tending the sick. Others carried the huge woven baskets of medicine bottles and supplies into the tents.

Abdullah charged around the outside of the boma, castigating the workers. Higher! It had to be higher, thicker, more tightly packed!

At high noon, Patterson, drenched in sweat, came to inspect the new hospital. He glanced up at Remington, who was strolling around the boma perimeter, his keen eyes taking in the work around him. The two men avoided each other.

The Masai graced the hills around the area, upright as trees as they stood on one leg, spear in hand, ever watchful of the slightest movement in the bush.

In the late afternoon, as soon as the hot sun began to drop, a huge bonfire was lit outside the new hospital.

THIRTY-NINE

Shadows and firelight flickered under a sky full of stars. And mayhem was waiting patiently in the grass beyond the thornbush.

Metallic sounds floated from within the boma around the officers' tent area.

Inside the closed boma, around a high, crackling fire, sat Patterson, Remington, Hawthorne, and Samuel, making their final preparations.

"I'll need you by me tomorrow," Remington said to Samuel.

"Whatever you wish," Samuel said quietly. His response was willing but notably flat—so different from the excitement the earlier lion hunt had elicited from the unfortunate Starling.

They were cleaning their guns religiously, as though to ward off evil.

Patterson's Holland .303 sporting rifle was a deadly, accurate gun, and he cleaned it expertly. He had hunted with it in India for many years and had brought in meat with it on several forays out into the Tsavo bush, not to mention the one-shot kill of the lion.

Remington's Rigby-Mauser, surprisingly, was the oldest. And the way his hands moved as he serviced it, he might have been bathing a child.

Hawthorne was the least skilled of the three. But his weapon was clearly the finest. A .450 Express. Bigger than the others, with great killing power.

As they were cleaning their guns, they heard purring. They all looked up.

It was Remington, purring like a cat, trying to unsettle the other three. He took a drink and pointed at Patterson. "Samuel says you killed a lion," he said.

"It was probably luck," Patterson said.

"Nobody ever got a lion with one shot by luck," Remington said. "You may be of use to me tomorrow. And even if you're not, I want you to understand something." He looked Patterson in the eye. "Even though it may take me two or three days to sort this out"—Patterson had to smile at the phrase—"when I'm gone, you'll still have to build the bridge," Remington said. "And I don't want the men to have lost respect for you."

Patterson was a bit surprised. "That's very considerate," he said.

"I'm always considerate," Remington said. "My mother taught me that."

Samuel broke out laughing.

"Why do you laugh?" Remington said. "You don't believe she taught me?"

"I don't believe you had a mother," Samuel said, chuckling.

Remington laughed too, then looked up. A Masai warrior who had materialized nearby was signaling to him. Remington nodded.

The warrior nodded in response and went back to where the others were.

The Masai had taken a place near a corner of the officers' tent area, and they had lit many fires. Now they started to sing what sounded like a battle chant.

Hawthorne watched them with grim fascination. He stood up and breathed deeply, trying to relax. He was terribly tense. Hawthorne was a doctor, not a hunter. Not once in his months out here had he taken his gun out in the bush to shoot. That Remington would invite his participation in the lion hunt meant only one thing: Even the fabled Remington found the situation critical.

But Remington had made it clear: The choice to join the hunt was Hawthorne's to make. Remington did not want a half-hearted shooter at his side.

"You're certain something will happen?" Hawthorne asked. He noted the barest nod from Remington. "But you're not excited," the doctor added.

It was clear Remington wasn't. He was stonefaced, as though indifferent to approaching danger; as though he'd seen so much death it was all in a day's work for him. He seemed almost without feelings.

"You don't enjoy killing, do you?" Patterson said.

Remington gave him a hard look that said, simply, No.

"Then why do it?" Hawthorne asked.

Remington stared in silence at his own flying hands as they finished reassembling the clean rifle parts. He stood up. "I have a gift," he said with a matter of fact shrug. Then he turned. "I must go and be with the Masai. We have to convince each other we're still brave."

"I wouldn't think bravery would be a problem for you," Hawthorne said. He was desperately seeking for *something* to believe in.

"You hope each time it won't be," Remington said. He looked out at the Masai. "But you never really know."

Patterson and the others watched as Remington strode away and joined the Masai.

Hawthorne's eyes followed the fabled hunter, their "savior." "Strange man," he said, almost to himself.

Patterson looked at Samuel. Samuel knew the American, knew the source of his strangeness.

"He lost," Samuel said, in response to Patterson's look. "The two great tribes of his country, they had a terrible battle, for many years."

"And his side lost?" Patterson said.

"More," Samuel said. "Land. And family . . . very young and very old . . . all lost."

The American Civil War. Remington had grown up in the deep South. He had lost his father and all his brothers and uncles by the time he was five. His mother was mercilessly degraded by Northen troops and hanged herself afterward. He was raised by his grandfather on his small plantation for a few years, until it was taken by Northern occupiers. They offered the old man and the boy work on the land. The grandfather died within six months, and the boy became a refugee in his own country.

"So he came here?" Hawthorne said.

Samuel watched the Masai and Remington for a moment. Remington had moved in among the tribesmen and was picking up their chant.

Samuel shook his head. "For years he hunted.

Alone," he said. "People heard. Someone sent for him."

They watched Remington beginning to move with his adopted clan as they chanted and swayed rhythmically.

"No reason ever to go back," Samuel said.

Hawthorne frowned. He had heard about this happening to certain white men out in the bush, how they could never come back. He had heard about it, but to a man fully intending to return to the comforts of civilization, the idea was foreign to him. He shrugged.

"John?" he said, turning to Patterson and holding out his beautiful weapon. "Change guns with me—mine's much more powerful. I'll be finishing the hospital so I won't be with you—but if you use this, then I can contribute something."

Hawthorne had made up his mind where he belonged during the hunt.

Touched by the offer, Patterson, exchanged weapons. "Thank you," he said. He took the .450 Express and admired it.

Hawthorne turned to Samuel. "Why does he need you by him?" he asked.

"He doesn't," Samuel said, watching the Masai. "He needs nobody. But we have hunted many times. He knows I am afraid of lions."

Samuel, an Akamba, accepted that he was different from both Remington and the Masai. He trailed off and moved toward the circle of their ceremony. It was louder suddenly, a full-blown war chant—with Remington, drinking, at the center of it all, by far the loudest chanter.

Remington and the Masai performed a cow-bleeding and blood-drinking ritual.

The Masai proceeded to go a little bit frenzied now as their bloodlust rose, the noise building, their bodies shaking in the firelight.

Patterson, standing alone in shadow, watched them.

Catching sight of him, Remington gestured for him to join them.

Paterson hesitated, shaking his head. Not yet. He stayed there in the shadows a long while, watching Remington laughing, drinking, and chanting with the Masai. He watched until they all began to paint their bodies in preparation for the hunt.

He turned and retreated to his own tent, to prepare in his own way.

But for the chanting and the sound of the drums, they all would have heard throaty rumbling drifting up from the hilly bushland south of the settlement. It was an agitated growl, almost as though in answer to the irksome din arising from the usually quiet lion buffet ground.

FORTY

At dawn, where the red lava rocks gave way to shady forest in the hilly bushland south of the Tsavo settlement, the fifty Masai gathered.

They carried their boldly painted war shields, round and oval, and behind the shields their long-bladed spears athwart or perpendicular.

The warriors had stark white slashes of paint up and down their faces. Spectacular ostrich-feather and lion-mane headdresses, halos of red, white, and brown adorned their pates. Lion- and leopard-tooth necklaces hung from their necks. These battle ornamentations, along with low humming chants and spear-feinting leaps, fought their fear and built their courage while they waited.

Patterson appeared from the direction of the camp, bleak-faced and unrested. It had been a long time since he had smiled. He carried Hawthorne's powerful rifle purposefully.

Samuel was already there, looking around anxiously.

Remington strode into view over a rise from the south and hurried his pace, clear-eyed and ready for anything.

The Masai moved in toward him. He spoke low and pointed. "I spotted one of them," he said. "In there." He gestured toward the copse—alternating thickets of thorn trees and taller canopy trees creating a dark environs, filled with long dawn shadows.

Remington, Patterson, and Samuel exchanged a look thick with tension.

"With any luck," Remington said, "I'll kill it in the thicket." He pointed Patterson in one direction. "Go around to the far end and find a position," he said. "Stay alert. Stay alert for anything."

"Warani," Remington said to the Masai. He made one hand gesture.

The warriors spread apart in one long line. As the sun began to rise through the trees, they started forward en masse, Remington on point.

Patterson, meanwhile, ran like hell as quietly as possible, to get to a cut-off position before contact was made.

The warriors, moving quickly and silently, covered the entire width of the copse.

Patterson came face to face with a thick cluster of thorn trees, ducked his head, and blasted through the thicket. He then stepped quickly over the rocky terrain and ran on.

Samuel, staying close to Remington, moved with him through the dappled forest. For Samuel, the fear was apparent in his wide-eyed visage. For Remington, it was impossible to tell. His face was an expressionless mask.

Remington, looking back and forth, kept track of the position of the warriors, who were ready.

Patterson, circling around the back now, picking up speed, was racing toward a distant clearing.

The *warani* spread out. The two powerful, brightly plumed and painted point men looked to Remington.

Remington signaled. Not yet.

Patterson raced into the clearing and glanced around. Anthills were everywhere. The African kind, eight feet high, casting long shadows across the ground.

Holding Hawthorne's marvelous rifle, Patterson slipped silently into the shadow of a giant anthill and stared deep into the dappled copse, trying to pick up a sign. Shaded from the bright morning sun, it was almost as if he wasn't there.

Remington, at the top of the copse, signaled.

The whole line of warriors suddenly shot forward.

Patterson lay in wait in the shadows.

Remington, moving forward, his eyes flicking into the thicket ahead, saw nothing. No movement at all. No lion.

The whole line of warriors started folding inward from the far ends. The two wildly colored, muscular point men moved slowly, their eyes locked on Remington.

For Samuel, with his long spear, the fear was almost incapacitating. He struggled to dog Remington's steps.

Remington, the big point men, and the approaching *warani* began to squeeze in on the densest part of the thicket in the little forest. There was still no movement from within.

The warriors slashed their way through with spears, cutlasses, making noise.

Remington was at their head, his eyes, as always, constantly scanning for any sign of life.

Remington stopped suddenly. He made a high-pitched bird sound because something *was* there.

One of the point men whistled in response.

In the thicket ahead, whatever Remington saw now began to move.

Out in the clearing, in the shadows, Patterson was invisible from the woods. He heard the whistle but saw nothing. He heard his own heart pounding and felt the hair on his arms begin to prickle in fear.

A flash of the Ghost appeared in the thicket, its eyes bright, agitated. Remington immediately spotted the shift and whistled to the warriors to go left.

The warriors, whistling back, shifted over as Remington directed, blocking the Ghost's intended path.

The Ghost, switching back, tried to go the other way this time.

Remington spotted the lion's movement, although it was just a ripple of light deep within the copse. He whistled for the warriors to shift the other way.

The warriors whistled in response and raced to their new position, blocking the animal's path again.

The Ghost, rattled, provoked, now started retreating back in the original direction.

Without warning, Remington suddenly started to scream, and instantly the whole long line of men was screaming too. It was as if mass hysteria had gripped them.

Patterson jumped, reacting to the din.

The warriors, beating shields and drums and shouting even louder in deafening whoops, pressed forward.

Remington broke into a dead run, screaming, rifle ready, toward the Ghost.

The two point men were also moving closer together, yelling at the tops of their voices.

The Ghost, confused and enraged, leapt out of sight.

Remington ran around a thicket and then stopped dead, shocked.

One of his point men was lying bloody on the ground.

Remington continued to move forward.

The second point man was also lying in a pool of blood, dead.

Yards deeper in the copse, the Ghost retreated steadily toward the clearing where Patterson waited.

FORTY-ONE

In the shadow of the anthill, Patterson held his breath.

The Ghost, beleaguered, tossed his head left, then right at the advancing, whooping lines of Masai, and backed through the woods. The huge mane flashed brilliantly in shafts of sunlight and then disappeared in shadow.

Patterson crouched in the clearing, eyes riveted, not breathing. The gigantic beast was backing right into his lap. Closer, closer, and closer still, as Patterson's face went stiff with terror.

The Ghost turned, and bared his God-awful incisors and roared.

Patterson, no more than ten yards from the enraged animal, had never seen anything so horrific. He froze by the anthill like a statue and couldn't even raise his rifle to a firing position.

The Ghost now saw Patterson.

In the woods, Remington was charging like hell, busting through the thorn thicket, trying to get into position.

Patterson was simply helpless.

The Ghost gathered himself to spring. For a moment, they were frozen in a horrible tableau.

Remington, dodging sideways through the trees, cursed violently. The anthills blocked him from getting a clear bead on the animal. He raced for a better angle, yelling, *"Shoot, for chrissakes!"*

The yell froze the Ghost for just two beats of the heart.

Just enough time for Remington, running, still without a clear shot, to fire anyway.

The bullet hit the ground between the Ghost and Patterson.

The Ghost reacted, staring at Patterson, splaying his front feet to redirect himself.

Patterson started, Remington's gunshot snapping him to at last. He raised his gun and squinted, the Ghost clear in his sights. He had him, this was it, this was the moment, and as he squeezed the trigger, a totally unexpected sound registered in his ears.

A dull snap.

Hawthorne's rifle had misfired.

And the Ghost, in a blur of amber, was gone.

Patterson stood bug-eyed in shock.

The silence fell like night.

Samuel, catching up to Remington, panted. "Did you ever see a lion that size?"

"Not even close," Remington said, moving intently toward Patterson. "What happened?" he asked.

Patterson spoke in a whisper. "Misfire," he said. "It jammed. . . ."

"Has it ever done that before?" Remington asked.

"Don't know," Patterson managed, struggling to keep his composure.

"It's Dr. Hawthorne's rifle," Samuel said, seeking to soften the blow for his friend.

Remington, also struggling to keep himself under control, took a long breath, and said, very low, "You exchanged weapons?"

Patterson nodded.

"You went into battle with an untried gun?" Remington said.

From Patterson, again a nod.

For a moment it was impossible to tell what Remington was going to do. A Homeric burst of fury seemed highly likely.

Patterson felt drained, expecting Remington's rage to break the quiet.

Instead, Remington studied the younger man. When he finally spoke, his voice was surprisingly quiet. "They have an expression in prizefighting," he said. " 'Everyone has a plan until they're hit.' You've just been hit. The getting up is up to you."

He turned away.

A Masai warrior stepped forward rather formally. Remington immediately gave him all his attention. The warrior spoke to him in Masai.

Samuel listened and began translating softly to Patterson: "They're leaving now because it does no good to be here. Two are dead, but it is more than that."

He paused and listened, then recited: "They are not lions. They are the Ghost and the Darkness. They'll kill us all if we stay."

Samuel's long, somber face was sick with dread.

FORTY-TWO

An eight-foot-high thorn boma now surrounded the new hospital.

Dr. Hawthorne, the orderlies, the African nursing crew, and all the hospital workers had gathered just inside the boma at Remington's request.

Patterson stood apart, still hearing the misfire dully clicking in his ears.

"Gentlemen," Remington said to some orderlies, "there is no sickness smell at all here and very little blood. We have removed all their temptations. When we leave, simply lock the gate securely and do not open it till morning. Keep your fires high. Questions?"

There were no questions, only subdued and sullen nods. Everyone understood, and no one believed.

They all knew that two of the most powerful of the Masai had been killed by a single lion that had then just slipped away without a scratch, despite all of the hunting rifles and all the long spears.

They all *knew* these were no mere lions, and were skeptical of the talkative Remington, who was only a mere man.

They were not safe, no matter how high the fires or

fences. The mighty Masai had quickly discovered the truth here in Tsavo: To leave it was to be safe. Those who had to stay in Tsavo would go to sleep in terror this night and as many nights as they lived, a fraction of an inch of canvas between themselves and raw, excruciating death.

To Samuel and Hawthorne, Remington said, "You two will sleep beautifully in your tents." Then, unnecessarily, *"And stay there."*

"And where will you two sleep beautifully?" Samuel asked, an urgency in his tone.

Remington smiled. "Mr. Patterson and I will be waiting for them in the old hospital. Won't we, Mr. Patterson?" he said. "Where the enticing smell of sickness still lingers."

Incredibly, Remington smiled. He was enjoying this. He led Patterson away. "And by the time we are done," he said to the engineer as they left the hospital boma and started down the hill, "I promise you this: The smell of fresh blood will be totally irresistible." He gave a harsh laugh and clapped Patterson on the back.

FORTY-THREE

At the old hospital, as dusk came on, Remington and Patterson carried buckets to spots around the outside of the canvas structure. Every ten paces or so, they dumped out a bucket. It was thick and dark as motor oil—blood.

They picked up huge chunks of raw meat and began scattering them by the building's doorways.

Out in the settlement, Samuel and Hawthorne hurried toward their camp, looking around in the gathering gloom. A shifting tree limb made them snap their heads. Every sound was enough to make their hearts stop.

At the old hospital, Patterson and Remington led three Masai cattle into the grounds of the hospital itself. They tied them up not far from the entrance flaps.

Inside the near-deserted space, the two men carried a hospital bed toward one of the eight-foot-high windows and placed it against the wall. Remington stood on it, looked out the window, and liked the view that he saw.

At the new hospital, the four orderlies firmly closed

and locked a heavy wooden gate across the opening in the boma. They hurried back to the sentry fires flanking the entrance and piled on more wood until the fires blazed high. Two of them moved inside and closed the door behind them. Two stayed out with the guns.

Patterson and Remington moved around inside the old hospital building, further baiting the trap by scattering more chunks of raw meat by the open doors and emptying more buckets of blood down the inside walls.

Outside, the light of day was fast dying.

Patterson and Remington emerged to light their own sentry fires, large ones, just outside the old hospital building. The flames soon leapt toward the sky. The two men separated to ignite more fires whose purpose was to light the whole building.

The new hospital was clean and full of patients with advanced and mortal diseases of the usual, knowable African kind: dysentery, Blackwater, snakebite, malaria. Diseases that were fearsome but in some way understandable. Not pure evil; not the work of the Devil. The "disease" roaming silently outside the hospital ripped your soul out first and ate it while you writhed in agony.

The hospital workers were exhausted from the frenzied work of the day. Most were already asleep, lions be hanged. The orderlies took shifts sitting by the fires outside the doors, alert for anything.

There were three doors to the old hospital building, and Patterson and Remington were closing them up now. The center door, however, they left slightly ajar, tying it shut with rope.

Just inside the door, and very visible in lantern light, the three Masai cattle were tied to a post close to the doorway. The cattle were quiet, oblivious to their purpose and probable fate.

Remington looked around the large room. What he had set up was a big fortified mousetrap, a garrison bristling with both bait and gun emplacements.

The windows now had beds underneath them for firing. The three cattle were tied together inside the main door in the middle. Chunks of raw meat were scattered inside the doorway.

Patterson, at one of the high windows, stared silently out at the moon.

"Think about something else," Remington said, reading Patterson's mind.

"Have you ever failed?" Patterson said without turning.

Remington gave a sad smile. "Only in life," he said. He walked away, humming "When Johnny Comes Marching Home." Patterson watched him wander across the big room.

About all Patterson knew of Remington was that he was a professional hunter sought by other professional hunters for tips or actual assistance.

That was so because Remington's knowledge ran deep. He had spent long months living by himself in the bush like a nomadic lion moving from territory to territory without a pride of his own.

During his solitary walkabouts he hunted for sustenance only and observed the habits of the game animals he made his living stalking.

From the beginning he was known as a skilled, thorough, and "clean" hunter. He never left an animal wounded, abandoning his client if necessary and tracking for miles to finish the job.

It was a vivid lesson he remembered from his boyhood in Mississippi. His grandfather largely raised him, and took the boy hunting hares and bobcat and boars starting at the age of seven.

One of the last summers of the old man's life, he had entrusted the boy, then ten years old, with putting his favorite and ailing plantation dog out of his misery. He was a soft-eyed black and white border collie.

Young Remington had steeled himself, gone down to the river with the dog, and botched the job. The dog looked at Remington with his soft eyes and dragged himself into the brush, suffering piteously. Remington ran. His grandfather had to finish the job.

The incident was never again mentioned. Remington went twelve years without picking up a gun, and when he did so again, in Africa, it was with the resolve never to fire it without utter mastery of the situation and himself.

He could bring down elephant with a single shot in the brain on a line from the eyeball to the ear opening. He started to become rich doing it for the ivory caravaners.

Very shortly he had sickened of it and turned to conducting safaris for European and American fat-cat big-game hunters.

But after a while he could only bring himself to allow the taking of old or lame lions and leopards and cheetahs, and only mature animals from the edge of big herds.

He stopped getting the best jobs and stopped getting rich. His bush knowledge grew and his income shrank. But he always managed to make enough to live and drink and fight in all the glittery watering holes from Brazzaville to Djibouti.

Remington had married once, disastrously.

He fell in love with a plump Irish widow who hired him on safari. Maura. She was young and rich and loved him for his wicked tongue and wild ways. They had in common a disdain for those not-so-rare European colonials who carried on like gods in places like Africa.

Maura scratched her leg on the iron flange of a baggage cart three weeks after they were married. She wanted to be as tough as he was for his sake, so she didn't mention it or put iodine on it. It gangrened when they were in the Congo a week later, and although she took her time about it, she died.

The truth was, Remington wasn't doing so well himself at the moment. He told no one, but something was eating his insides. He suspected he was full of hookworm. He sure as hell wasn't going to lie down for any doctoring for it, though, other than an administration of good German whiskey.

FORTY-FOUR

Patterson's new tent area had been set up by the African village. Hawthorne's smaller tent was nearby in the same compound. Hawthorne sat by the large fire near his tent and shivered.

Samuel watched him, feeling for once that the white man was not so different from the African. Nervously, they drank tea.

On his cot platform in the old hospital, Patterson watched the moon rise higher.

An hour passed. Then another. Patterson preferred the small, high windows on the moon end of the building, because from this vantage point, with the pale silver moonlight painting the ground and the thorn trees, he could see everything.

Remington walked along the far end of the abandoned, smelly tent, his rifle ready.

Patterson moved over to the agitated cows in the center of the room, patting their flanks, speaking quietly to them.

Outside the doors of the old hospital, the large chunks of meat glistened in the moonlight.

Nothing disturbed the peace at the new hospital. The orderlies were calm.

Outside their boma, the guards could see orange fires glowing through the night mist all across the settlement.

Beyond the encampment, the river palms shuddered in the warm wind and the Pathans clucked to each other in their shelters erected on the finished part of the bridge. The only sounds coming to the orderlies were the barking of wild dogs and the intermittent squawks of gray parrots talking to each other in the fever trees.

Remington stopped in the flickering lantern light in the middle of the old hospital and studied Patterson. The young engineer, once so impeccable and now so haggard, leaned against the tent pole and stared out his window with febrile eyes. The man clearly craved redemption.

Remington eased over near him. "Meant to ask you," he said. "The railroad-car trap. Your idea?"

Patterson nodded.

"Excellent notion," Remington said. "I used the same device myself once."

"But of course yours worked," Patterson said.

"In point of fact, it didn't," Remington said. "But I'm convinced the idea is sound. As you can see, I've refined it for this evening."

A humane gesture, meant to reassure and bolster the good man's courage.

At the back of Remington's gesture was the knowledge they could ill afford any more episodes of paralysis like the one in the copse. Patterson could shoot. He needed to shoot if they were going to survive this war. Remington went back to walking the edge of the room.

Patterson watched him, and as he did, Remington's gesture seemed to work. For the first time since the misfire, his mood began to lift.

The orderlies at the new hospital had begun to relax. Their fires were high, their bomas gleamed strong in the firelight. Their fresh-smelling digs felt secure.

The sick and injured woke and groaned and needed care. The orderlies tended to them quietly.

Remington stalked the big room at the old hospital, keeping himself alert. No sound from outside, not even the cries of the fish-eagles by the river. The night had grown deadly quiet.

Patterson leaned at the other end of the room. And suddenly a different and frightening sound filled the air: the ripping of flesh. Right outside Patterson's window.

The shadows of two massive forms moved over the ceiling.

Remington moved quickly across and gestured for Patterson to switch positions with him.

As he reached where Patterson was and was about to mount the cot, the eating sound stopped.

Silence again.

Patterson reached the far end of the building.

Then the eating sound came again, and now both lions could be heard outside Patterson's new window.

Another piece of the fresh, glistening red meat was ripped away by a huge claw.

Remington looked across at Patterson. Whatever was going on outside, it was sure as hell odd.

Patterson climbed quietly onto the bed by the window, rifle ready, peering out. From his face Remington could tell there was nothing to see.

The cattle were becoming agitated. One of them kicked out violently against the smell in the night—the same gesture the cattle did just before the Ghost walked through their *kraal* by the water hole and killed one.

Then a different sound was heard: *scratching*. And it was coming from underneath the building.

Remington hurried to where the sound was.

Patterson, still standing up on the bed, turned to watch Remington. As he did, a lion's head flashed in the window, and a claw crashed through the opening, ripping at Patterson's head.

Patterson cried out as he felt the fanned air. He spun back toward the window, raising his rifle. The window was empty.

Remington waited where the sound had come from underneath the building. How could they get under the floor?!

Silence.

Then a new sound was heard—coming from the corrugated tin roof above.

Patterson moved to Remington's side. They waited, looking up, guns poised. Silence. They heard no more sounds beyond the pounding of their hearts.

Patterson fidgeted, frustrated. Remington, however, seemed quite content.

Then the main door, the one that had been left

slightly ajar and tied, began to move. Remington and Patterson edged silently across from the door.

The rope lashing the narrow handles of the open door looked liable to give way at any instant.

The cattle, near the door, began to snort, kicking, yanking at their bridles.

Remington and Patterson waited. From the look on Remington's face, this was it. The doors bulged inward. Patterson raised his rifle.

The cattle were now screaming from fright, lion scent washing over them.

Suddenly, there was no pressure against the door at all. The doors hung loose. The man-eaters were gone.

Remington and Patterson stood there. Patterson was furious. "Goddammit!" he said.

"It's all right," Remington said. "Stay ready." He indicated the blood poured down the walls and door. "They know it's there."

Remington gestured to Patterson to open the door.

Patterson carefully moved forward, untied the ropes, pulled the doors slowly open. Remington moved silently beside him. They stared out into nothing but darkness. They stepped back into shadow and waited.

FORTY-FIVE

At the new hospital, a guard-orderly, blood pouring from his throat, lay by the sentry fire. No signs of struggle, just a throat ripped out by one swipe of claws.

The second orderly rounded a corner. Seeing the savagery, he opened his mouth to scream, but before he could—

The Ghost and the Darkness both suddenly leapt all over him, their giant paws slapping out so fast the second orderly could not follow the course of the blows that killed him.

He dropped to the ground.

Then the whole place spun into madness. Like lightning, a tent full of sick men with malaria and Blackwater and dysentery turned into an abattoir.

A paw flashed and blood flew, with never so much as a groan. The sick man, an Indian, fell from his bed, blood pouring from his slashed face.

The Darkness, lips pulled back over bloodied fangs, leapt over that victim onto the next.

Two more sick men, trying to rise, fell back, parts of their faces missing.

158

The Ghost, leaping onward, bloody flesh falling from his jaws, was not killing to eat. He was killing to slake some primal madness.

The Darkness, standing with front paws on the chest of a dead invalid, jerked his narrow and brilliant eyes toward the sick worker on the corner cot who was starting to scream.

The sound just barely escaped him before he was dead.

But scream he did, with his last breath, the first cry overheard from the whirlwind of blood.

The entire Tsavo camp stretched out before the new hospital, down the gentle slope. All the fires were burning. Patterson's old tent area was close by but not his new one. And the old hospital was on the other end, a good distance away.

Paterson and Remington were waiting, rifles ready. But no scream reached them, no sound at all.

Hawthorne, however, close by in his tent, heard the stifled scream and was up and finding his rifle and running out. Samuel did his best to stop him before he reached the gate.

"We must not leave," he said.

"That's my hospital, for God's sake," Hawthorne said, ripping free. His cynicism had its limits. He could not dismiss his patients like so much raw meat.

The main hospital tent was half pulled down. A second tent started to collapse as the Ghost and the Darkness sprung across into the medicine tent.

A frenzy of powerful leaps and slashing paws sent medicine flying across the tent. Glass shattered as more medicine was destroyed. The tent was just a blizzard of lions' claws and lions' teeth on fabric and flesh, along with those terrible, bright, blazing yellow eyes.

Another tent pole was pulled out of the ground and the action was unmistakable: The Ghost and the Darkness were destroying the new hospital piecemeal, systematically, with uncanny intent.

More hospital tents collapsed in the jaws and scything swipes of the man-eaters. They were absolutely insane with bloodlust, their eyes crazed, their huge heads thrown wildly.

Hawthorne, alone in the night and scared shitless, came at a dead run.

Moving shadows suddenly jumped out at him. He recoiled and ran on, starting up the rise. His heart was pounding as he looked up ahead.

He gasped: Two large eyes were staring at him. Yellow agate eyes. He veered, panicked, stumbling, falling, rolling over. Getting up, he stared back around.

The yellow eyes were gone. Disappeared without a trace.

Then there were more loud shrieks on the night air, coming from the area of the new hospital.

Remington and Patterson at last heard the shouts. Throwing the gate to the old hospital open, they took off, their rifles at the ready.

Hawthorne ran toward the new hospital just ahead.

Patterson and Remington tore through the night toward him.

Hawthorne ran through the entrance break in the boma fence around the new hospital. The tents were all askew or flattened, and the place was devastated.

Hawthorne pushed his way inside the first tent in disbelief. It was filled with the dead and the dying.

160

Grievous wounds on limbs and necks. Sprays of blood and flesh on tent walls.

The blood drained from his face. Carnage so complete there was nothing he could do. He pushed canvas out of his way and staggered on.

He moved along under the half-collapsed ceiling of the tent. More dead, more appallingly gashed and bleeding patients and orderlies. These were machines of evil, Hawthorne now knew, more full of foul intent than mere animals were capable of.

In the second tent, more dead. More dying. A slaughterhouse. Hawthorne was crushed. He fought for breath. His body sagged. He steadied himself against a pole and took a breath—his last.

The Ghost and the Darkness were on him, *roaring*.

Patterson and Remington, pounding up the rise, heard the roar just as the new hospital was about to come into view. They glanced at each other, then they slowed.

They were looking at the spot where the new hospital had been.

Remington stared at the butchery. A look of infinite sorrow crossed his face. For a moment it seemed he was about to fall, his body drained of all its power. He swayed, trying not to topple, unable to move.

Patterson moved deliberately into the hospital area. And entered into the heart of chaos.

He stared around. The dead and the dying were everywhere. Hawthorne, his face clawed almost unrecognizably, lay alone.

All that was left now was the sound of pain.

FORTY-SIX

From across the tracks came an Indian worker carrying a bundle of possessions, running for the station as though for his life. Tied together in his bundle were his tent, his tools, his blanket, and his cooking pots. He was hurrying to join his countrymen.

At the Tsavo station, the red dust swirled and covered everything. Only the sound was more enveloping than the dust. An incredible babble of human voices rose up from the station. The platform was jammed with people hurrying up and people already waiting.

A sea of white cotton. At least half the contracted Indian labor force was congregated. The fate of the Uganda Line bridge-building/permanent-way project was written in the excitement on their faces, in the intensity of their new resolve.

They were set to leave what had become a place of death. Kali, the Destroyer, had unleashed her dogs here. No contract was strong enough to keep them. No amount of rupees made staying—and ending one's time in the belly of a lion—worthwhile.

They craned their necks down the track that looped back around the settlement, the turnaround spur.

They could hear the chuffing of the Mombasa material train coming around toward the loading platform.

Patterson walked up through the red dust, estimating the numbers at the station. Samuel, a worried look on his face, was a few steps behind. Patterson was valiantly hoping for only a small-scale defection, but he could not shake a sense of doom. His sense was right.

The Mombasa train came into view and pulled into the station, only you almost couldn't tell it was a train. It was already so jammed with workers who had climbed on before the station, it was hard to see how the multitudes on the platform would be able to squeeze on board.

Now a new wave hit the train and it virtually disappeared where it stood. All one could see were the workers scrambling up the sides of the cars, clambering up onto the roofs, onto the engine, the cowcatcher—covering every inch of the train.

The Pathans, Punjabis, Muslims, Hindus, Sikhs—the entire expatriot Indian work force of over four hundred men was now on the train with all their bundled possessions.

Everyone was leaving.

Patterson could only watch. He could not even place any blame, although this meant for him supreme failure. For added to their bundles, the workers also carried away Tsavo's dire reputation, and their stories told in Voi and Mombasa and Bombay would deny Patterson any hope of a replacement work force.

Abdullah stood on top of one of the cars as the train began to pull out of the station.

More and more workers chased after it and were

pulled on board. The marvel was that the boxcars and flatcars didn't simply topple over from the teeming humanity clinging and crawling over them.

Patterson still watched, his eyes vacant.

Abdullah saw him, and looked away.

The train gathered speed. It grew smaller and lost its solidity in the shimmering heat waves. It rounded a corner and was gone.

The Tsavo station was empty, the platform deserted. Even the native *askari*—the watchful armed guards with repeating rifles—had abandoned the walkways of the fortified water tower. There was little left to guard. The red dust began to settle.

Patterson turned from the scene and began to walk away. Samuel stayed close behind him, an anxious look on his face, not at all sure what his friend would do.

Patterson walked back along the rail tracks in silence. His failure was absolute. He had not been able to command the loyalty of his men. His accomplishment would be measured in the graves of Indian laborers and the pathetic truncated limb of a bridge broken off halfway across the Tsavo.

He would soon be a joke, he knew, in the Foreign Office outposts and cocktail verandas up and down British Africa and out east. In The City in London and in Whitehall, he would be vilified—a criminally incompetent impediment to Empire and a comfort to Her Majesty's enemies. The responsibility he had welcomed so avidly now ground down on him with pitiless force.

He made his way past the old hospital in the background toward the devastated new hospital. He looked inside. A few African orderlies did the best they could. Patterson watched only for a moment, then walked on, with Samuel still behind him.

The camp was a ghost town. Patterson walked through and made his inventory. Only about three dozen men remained: African workers, a few *askari*, and fifteen Indian laborers too sick to make the train.

Patterson was now powerless against the man-eaters. He would not be able to advance the bridge an inch. For what purpose should he stay? To take Beaumont's broadsides?

As they neared Patterson's new tent by the African village, Samuel darted into the tent and emerged with something, which he held out to Patterson.

It was the necklace of lion claws he had given him earlier.

"One of us needs to be brave," Samuel said.

Patterson made an almost courtly bow of thanks, put it on, and resolved never to take it off again. He walked on alone now, his face a grim mask.

FORTY-SEVEN

The grassy field on the far side of the bridge rippled in the late-afternoon sun.

Remington moved slowly through the grass, studying the ground. His face was dark with unaccustomed feelings.

Patterson approached.

Remington spoke out of the blue, without looking up. "It would have been a beautiful bridge, John," he said. "I never noticed it before, occupied with other business, I suppose." He rambled on as he walked. "Never really pay much attention to that kind of thing.... But I've had the time today, nothing else on, and this ... It's graceful, and the placement couldn't be prettier ... and ..."

He went off in silence, staring across the waving grass in the direction of the lowering sun.

Patterson watched him. "You just got hit," he said.

Remington nodded.

"The getting up is up to you," Patterson said. "And they're only lions."

Remington heard himself talking. He knew Patterson wasn't mocking him, only trying to give him

166

back his strength. "Yes, I saw fresh paw prints," he said, pointing. "Heading that way." He looked at Patterson. "We've both been hit."

"Let's go after them," Patterson said.

The two men made their way toward distant rocky high cliffs, one of the massive granite outcroppings that jut from the central African plain, thrown up over the eons by the earth's crust folding and the volcanic action of the Great Rift Valley not far to the west.

This *kopje* was hundreds of feet tall, stark and gorgeous in the morning light.

Patterson and Remington had tracked across several miles of grass and bushland, following the scats and the distinctive scarred pugs of the giant, black-maned lion.

At the edge of a rocky swale, they had found a place where the lions had stopped to eat. All that was left of the kill was the calf and foot still in the boot of one of the Indian stone workers taken from the hospital.

They went on, following lion signs and leavings. A bit of cotton loincloth on thornbush; a tangle of blue viscera and a shin bone in a nullah where another meal had been taken.

Now they reached the foot of the high *kopje* and tracked the pugs up a sloping ledge that made a natural ramp up the cliff face. They worked their way higher up along the rock face.

Patterson was much more nimble. It was dangerous, of course, but neither of them had that uppermost in mind. They traveled lightly, equipped with only small knapsacks and their weapons.

The two of them clambered over the rock face, tracking as they went. More scats, bones, a white turban, a copper bracelet of the sort the Indian laborers wore for good health left a trail of death.

They reached a rocky ledge and turned and stood. They stared out over the midday savanna.

They saw the world.

A sun and sky white with heat, and below it, unending miles of African highland. On the grasslands, hundreds of scattered herds all drifting southward on their great annual trek: zebras, wildebeests, elands, topis, Thomson's gazelles, giraffes, cape buffalo. Elephants in droves. Flights of birds. Prides of lazy lions. Wheeling vultures.

They beheld the richness of a world not of man's making.

Patterson and Remington looked for a long while, unable to turn away. Finally they turned their backs and moved on.

They were climbing along the edge. It was tricky going, and if they fell, they wouldn't live to tell. They were both concentrating on their movements, paying no attention to each other, as Remington started to speak.

"In my town, when I was little," he said as they climbed, "there was a brute, a bully who terrorized the place. But he was not the problem. He had a brother who was worse than he was. But the brother was not the problem either. One or the other of them was usually in jail. The problem came when they were both free together. The two became different from either alone. Alone they were only brutes. Together they became lethal; together they killed."

"What happened to them?" Patterson asked after a moment.

"I got big," Remington said.

They kept on climbing, and as the dongas began to level out near the top, Patterson and Remington worked their way around a steep ravine where it was hard going. They took pains to help each other.

Moving along the edge of the ravine, slowly, silently, they came in view of a rock overhang blocked by a tangled thicket of bushes and thorns.

Remington stopped and signaled silence, pointing to the thicket. One odd thing about it: There was a clearly defined archway, as if a buffalo or rhino used it as a regular passage.

The two of them moved up to the archway. They looked at each other and, without a word, raised their rifles and passed through it.

Between the thicket and the rock wall was a clearing, and in the rock wall, a cave.

The cave mouth was dark from across the clearing. Remington and Patterson checked their guns and moved across the clearing toward it.

As they approached the cave mouth, it suddenly seemed eerie. It was pitch black inside the cave. They couldn't see two feet within. It could have been the pathway to Hades. Remington moved slowly up to it, Patterson right with him.

Remington squinted inside. What slowly took shape was dark and dangerous—a long low tunnel they would have to half-crawl through.

Without discussion or hesitation, they got down and started inside, moving as stealthily as possible.

The first part of the cavern past the tunnel was colossal.

Patterson and Remington moved with quiet care, pressing deeper into the angled cave. Around a sharp bend, it got terrifyingly dark, except for spooky barbs of light coming from cracks in the rock, lighting some corners, totally obscuring others. It was dank. It felt as if, at any moment, the world could end.

Remington stopped, lowered his rifle, and stared, thunderstruck. "Dear God," he muttered.

Patterson looked.

On the floor of the cave were more copper bracelets. And still more. But that wasn't what Remington was reacting to.

It was the bones. The floor of the place was littered with human bones. Eyeless skulls peered up at them from all around.

Then the rest of the cave opened up around the next turning. They were looking at a carpet of bones.

Remington, an Africa hand all his adult life, had hunted and been hunted by all the predators. He knew their habits. Of the big cats, you might find leopards and cheetahs ensconced in lairs. But lions were open-plains dwellers. They slept by day in the sun on a rise of ground or on the shoulder of a *kopje*. Not in caves. They dragged their kills into the lee of an outcropping or just settled down to feast on the grassy plain. Lions just didn't have lairs like this.

Remington was freaked.

Patterson had had enough of the place. He turned

to go. "We might as well go back," he said. "They'll smell we've been here."

"I know," Remington said. "They'll never return." He was experiencing a flush of deep anxiety about these man-eaters. "They're doing it for pleasure," he said.

FORTY-EIGHT

They worked in their tents in the greatly reduced officers' compound located by the African village.

Patterson wrote in his journal, documenting his failure, chewing over the humiliation in store for him when Beaumont returned. He tormented himself with the fantasy that the entire rail line from Mombasa to Ugowe Bay on Lake Victoria would be completed sometime the year after the next, and the one link still unfinished would be his. He would be derided in Parliament and caricatured by Fleet Street.

In fact, he knew, he would be cashiered shortly and someone else would come and finish the bridge.

And all that paled in importance to the disgrace he would take home to Helena and the shame his son would have to live with.

Patterson, Remington, and Samuel heard it at the same time. Outside the thorn fence came a sickening sound: the crunching of bones.

The men shot out of their tents and listened. Patterson was on one side of the area, Remington and Samuel on the other.

"Both of them," Samuel said. He was pointing in the direction of Patterson's old tent area.

"Both over there," Remington said, nodding. He crossed to Patterson.

Patterson had squatted down and was sketching a small model of a *machan* in the dirt. "Ever have to use a *machan?*" he asked.

"Sounds like something else you've learned in India," Remington said.

The sketch represented four long slender poles stuck into the ground angled inward, with a plank across the top. Rather primitive.

Patterson, drawing a circle around his model, said, "They're used to people in trees, not in a clearing." He poked at the plank across the top. "It may be tight."

"Not for me," Remington said without blinking an eye. "It's your idea, you go up there."

"I'll be bait alone?" Patterson said with a touch of irony.

"Yes, and I'll be in a distant tree where I can provide no assistance whatsoever," Remington said with the same irony. He looked Patterson over. "Can you control your fear?"

"I'll have to," Patterson said.

Patterson built his *machan,* exactly as he remembered it from the hill village in northwest India where the headman had put himself out as bait for tiger. That poor man had died. God willing, Patterson would be luckier.

With help from Samuel and Remington, he buried the ends of four twelve-foot poles in the ground at

173

the corners of a square. Between the tops of the poles he lashed a sturdy plank reachable only by ladder. That was all there was to it.

Samuel brought in an ornery, spitting baboon and tied it to the base of one of the legs of the *machan*.

Patterson and Remington completed their work and were examining the ungainly thing.

"Lions hate baboons," Samuel said.

"Anything to add to your evening's pleasure," Remington said.

Patterson took a look at the baboon, then up at the plank. He tested the support poles. They were extremely rickety. The very slightness of the structure was the idea. The lion would see nothing to fear in a few spindly saplings in a clearing.

Remington held a wooden ladder propped against the plank. Patterson climbed his slow way up. It was a shaky contraption. He made it to the top, clambered off the ladder, managed to sit. They handed him his .303 carbine, then removed the ladder; no telling what these ungodly man-eaters were capable of.

The view from up there was frightening. There was nothing around the *machan*. Patterson felt like a pickle on a plate, served up for bestial delectation. Totally vulnerable. He began to have second thoughts just as Samuel carried away the ladder.

Patterson tried to get comfortable. He couldn't. This was a desperate idea, not a smart one. He was getting close to panicking.

Remington, watching him, suddenly looked all around and said, "It's certainly the best chance they've had to kill you." His remark was meant both to fortify through humor and to give recognition to Patterson's supreme bravery.

It registered with Patterson. His heart jumped at first, then he forced himself to get control. This *was* his moment—a chance for redemption. He might not have another. Finally he nodded. Remington started to leave.

"How many do you think they've killed?" Patterson asked compulsively.

Remington answered reluctantly. "The most of any lions," he said. "A hundred. Probably more." He handed Patterson his *houda*. "Don't worry, I have a feeling this is going to work."

"Why?" Patterson asked.

Remington shrugged. "Because I think they're after you." He gave Patterson a look and started away, then stopped. "Oh . . . Merry Christmas."

"What?" Patterson said, stunned.

"It's this month, I think," he said. He paused, then looked up at the younger man. "Johnny?"

They studied each other in the gathering darkness. They'd been through a lot together, these two. They were not what they had been when they first met. An emotional moment was clearly at hand.

"Don't fuck up," Remington said, and he turned to go, never looking back.

FORTY-NINE

In the late afternoon, with the sun about to die, before
the rank mists formed on the green, sluggish river,
Remington positioned himself in a tall tree. He was
back away from the clearing, but with rifle in hand
and clear sight lines to the *machan*.

He angled himself toward Patterson perched on the
stilts. He propped his rifle across his body and sighted
in on the nervous baboon across the broad clearing.
He wasn't that far away after all. He had the setup
covered. He cradled his rifle and waited.

The sun died. The hunting and feeding hour began.

In the silence and near dark of late dusk before the
hunting calls and cries began, Remington and Patterson were both in position, ready for whatever
happened.

Except what did happen.

Fog began rolling in. Thick river fog, getting denser
as the sky darkened.

Remington in his tree suddenly realized it. "Shit shit
shit," he muttered, anger suffusing his face.

The same anger was washing over Patterson.

Twelve feet up on his *machan*, he sat uncomfortably

176

ready as the silence extended, listening for something, *anything*.

But all there was was silence and the rolling fog. Soon he would be suspended in a sea of fog.

The baboon began screaming eerie, intermittent protests.

Patterson, looking around, was getting the urge to scream too. He could no longer see even the bushes bordering the clearing. The fog was impenetrable.

In his tree, Remington cursed, trying to keep the *machan* in focus through the gray. He would see it, then lose it. Finally it disappeared altogether.

Neither of them saw the white-maned lion come stalking, his belly low, through the bush to the edge of the clearing.

The Ghost held still. And with his lion eyes—the largest eyes of any meat-hunting animal—he saw as a lion sees: no colors, only tones, shades of gray, white, black. He clearly saw the baboon through the fog, tied at the foot of the *machan*. The piercing shrieks of the baboon, thunderous to him, begged the swipe of a silencing claw.

The Ghost kept his eyes fixed on the baboon. Patient, judging the risk, he waited for signs of danger. Waiting for the upright animal to tip his hand if he was lurking nearby.

Patterson had no inkling the lion was there. He scanned around with his eyes and saw nothing. Even sounds were muted by the choking fog. Now and then he thought he saw the outline of the thorn bushes.

The Ghost began to flow like oil out into the clearing, toward the baboon. Closer . . . just the barest few steps closer . . .

Patterson sensed something in the change in tone of the baboon's screams. A quality of strain, of terror. But he could see nothing, not even the baboon now. But the Ghost saw the baboon, very clearly and very very close.

Patterson heard the baboon stop screaming in midscreech.

He searched below him with his eyes, squinting desperately at the area around the baboon, but the mist was so thick he couldn't be certain of anything. He tried to turn around on the *machan* to see the baboon but couldn't. He sensed something horrible was about to happen.

Remington, in his tree, reacted to the sudden silence of the baboon. He knew absolutely what it meant. He strained his eyes and saw nothing. The mist obscured everything. He slowly, quietly, began to make his way down the tree. He had to get closer to Patterson.

What the Ghost saw over the broken-necked body of the baboon was the piece of leather where the animal was attached to the pole. He clamped his jaws on the baboon and gave a tentative pull.

On the narrow platform, Patterson, seeing nothing, hearing nothing, felt the pull and could barely breathe for fear. He locked his free hand on the plank.

The Ghost now saw the other four legs of the platform. He gave powerful jerks on the baboon carcass. All the legs moved and the platform began to sway.

The Ghost's eyes traveled up the platform, where the four legs drew closer together. At last he saw Patterson. His agate eyes narrowed. He backed up, yanking at the baboon. The slender legs of the *machan* swayed toward him, pulling the structure off vertical.

Patterson, blind to what was going on below, holding on for dear life, had no way of aiming his weapon. Suddenly the pressure released and the *machan* returned to upright.

The lion loosed his jaws and backed away from the baboon pace by pace, watching the struggling man through the gray of the fog.

Now the mist swirled and thinned momentarily below the *machan*, but all Patterson saw was the inert form of the baboon still tethered to the stilt. The fog closed up again.

The Ghost, never taking his eyes off the gray-toned prey above him, began to move. The angle shifted as he circled, silent as the fog, moving in and out of the edge of the bush.

Patterson, unseeing, putting all his sensing power in his ears, somehow heard a kind of whisper—the sound of animal flanks brushing bushes, now there at his right, moving, now behind him. He half turned the other way, trying not to have anything behind him.

The Ghost saw Patterson shifting as he continued to circle beneath the *machan.*

The realization hit Patterson and he flushed all over: The beast was stalking him. He was the prey.

A lion, incredibly strong in the haunches, could leap thirty-five feet through the air. Patterson knew he was anything but safe. He was not out of the reach of the man-eater's claws.

The Ghost circled, watching the platform, drawing in closer.

Patterson's heart was pounding so hard he was feeling the nausea of terror, this beast circling and circling, always closer, never visible. His throat was burning dry, and he was dying to let go a blast with his weapon or scream for it to do—anything! Anything but this constant circling, stalking . . .

The Ghost sensed the helplessness and began to tighten his circle.

Patterson, trying to turn on his shaky plank, lost track of the whispered sound and tried to pick up the animal's shifting position.

The man-eater saw the prey's confusion and sensed the kill.

Patterson, staring at the goddamn mist, was about to come apart with the tension building and building.

The Ghost moved closer.

Patterson gripped his weapon tightly as his head kept on turning.

There was a sudden fluttering and flapping. Patterson yelled out loud as an *owl* landed on him. That's right, a bloody owl landed on him, thinking he was a tree, almost knocking him off the plank.

The lion saw Patterson start to slip off the platform. He drew his legs under him, ready to pounce.

Remington was now moving fast through the fog toward the center of the clearing.

The Ghost watched Patterson sliding, grasping at the platform, about to fall. He coiled. . . .

Patterson, holding on with one hand, rifle in the other, swiped at his head, trying to fight the owl away. His balance was going, and he was sliding, trying like hell not to fall.

The lion crept forward as Patterson started to fall, getting ready to spring. . . .

Patterson slipped completely off and was falling. . . .

The Ghost was just starting its leap when Remington materialized in the fog, aiming.

Patterson hit the ground, and the Ghost bounded toward him. Remington couldn't shoot because Patterson was in the way. Patterson rolled over and fired his rifle.

The Ghost in midair let out an incredible roar and spun, and landed hard. He was hit, but he could still move, and with one gigantic leap he was gone.

FIFTY

The sun rising red over the Tsavo bush tried to break through the morning mist, but all it did was make the world look bloody.

Remington and Patterson moved forward in the gleaming haze, half blind, close together, hunting cautiously. Strange shapes loomed up around them as they searched for the place where the old lion had gone to hide.

The Ghost was watching.

What he saw was Patterson and Remington moving through a field of giant anthills. He was watching them from above, not that far away from them. In fact, as Patterson and Remington crept among the anthills, barely making a sound, the Ghost was practically above them.

Remington squinted around desperately. Patterson did the same. But neither of them had the right angle of elevation. What they didn't know was that no more than twenty paces up ahead, high on an anthill, crouched and ready, was the Ghost.

The two men took another step.

The Ghost watched the tonal shapes approaching through the shining, blinding morning haze. Closer . . .

Patterson and Remington stopped. They stood there, close together, frozen.

There was total silence now. The mist muffled everything, leaving no sign of lion.

Yet the men were certain the man-eater was in here. The profuse blood trail had led through scrub jungle and a grove of fig trees along the river straight to this unearthly spot. In the lee of a lava outcropping they found a darkened pool where the wounded predator had lain the night and vomited. The trail leading away from it was still fresh.

A strange feeling washed over Remington. He put out a hand to stop Patterson. The lion was going to attack, he knew it. Patterson knew it too. They just didn't know where.

The Ghost looked down at Remington and Patterson, who were glancing all around them.

Sets of muscles rippled along the Ghost's flanks as in one motion he gathered himself and sprang.

Before Patterson or Remington expected anything, the Ghost had launched himself into the air.

But even then, it was too late.

Because Remington, by reflex, spun and fired.

And as the sound exploded, the Ghost twisted in midair, his chest exploding in a red spray, and fell. Thudding shamefully to the ground, he rolled once and rose, roaring blood, charging.

Remington fired his rifle twice more into the bloodied chest. The Ghost pulled up, legs splayed apart as though he had lost his sense of balance, and fell sideways, raking the chalky dirt into the air with his claws, and died.

FIFTY-ONE

A sudden flash of light. It was the pop of a flashbulb.

The foppish young photographer in a white linen suit and bowtie was up from Mombasa. He pulled out a photographic plate and shoved in a new one.

His even younger assistant, wearing a suit, straw boater, and rakishly thin mustache, readied another flash tray while standing guard over a load of bulky equipment.

Patterson and Remington milled around behind the photographer, watching the man and his subjects.

A lovely setting for it, under green ferns and river palms by the swollen, flowing Tsavo.

It was plain Remington and Patterson had been drinking. Remington tried to pass Patterson the champagne bottle. Patterson was half-heartedly cleaned up in his military-style cotton drills for the occasion. He passed on the champagne; he'd had enough for the nonce.

Remington drank for him. He had regained much of his seen-it-all swagger.

One of the photographer's subjects was done up with pith helmet and big-game rifle: Beaumont. He had been reached by telegraph at the temporary rail-head at Simba. He had trained straight down the line upon hearing the news.

"I think another for posterity," he said. "This is an important moment in my life."

He struck another pose. The photographer went to work, arranging the man's limbs and the overhanging foliage.

"Understand, I had help," Beaumont said.

"Not a time for modesty, Bob," Patterson said with an absolutely straight face.

"Undeniably your triumph," Remington said, just on the edge of snorting with laughter. He was not so much unimpressed by Beaumont as just plain scornful. Remington lived the life of a bushman just to escape such types.

Beaumont was oblivious. "Oh surely there's enough credit for us all," he said, while the photographer moved his head around, searching for the right jut of chin. "Let's not forget, you did the actual shooting. Of course, *I* hired you, *I* was the general who put the team together. And generals are the ones who tend to be remembered."

The photographer, struck by inspiration, said to Beaumont enthusiastically, "Perhaps you could put your head in its mouth, sir. Could be a corker."

"Clever idea," Beaumont said with his famous smile, his red, pomaded Kaiser mustache bobbing. "I like it."

He turned to the other photographic subject: the white-maned Ghost. The war-scarred old lion had been laid out on the length of a supply cart. His shoulders were propped up by a board for proper effect.

His wildly maned head was held up with sticks. He had been stretched out his full ten feet.

The mouth of the Ghost was huge. Beaumont and the photographer together just managed to get it open. Beaumont, though he was a touch nervous and trying to hide it, with a show of forthright boldness put his head between the enormous sets of teeth.

Whereupon Remington gave a sudden loud imitation of a lion's roar, and Beaumont, badly startled, jerked his head away.

Raucous laughter erupted from both Remington and Patterson. Patterson took the champagne bottle from Remington and drank in salute.

Beaumont tried for his famous smile but couldn't bring it off. He looked around, humiliated, as the laughter rolled from other onlookers.

FIFTY-TWO

Patterson and Remington drank into the night by their tents near the African-village area.

Samuel wandered over to the two men by the fire and took Patterson's offer of a champagne bottle. It was a sweet moment of victory for these men, their first, with no fear in the vicinity.

Remington's long stringy hair hung from under his bush hat, his buffalo-hide vest was stained with blood, and his smile was wide.

Patterson's momentary spiffiness at the ritual photographing of the kill had given way to what was now the real Patterson—a world away from the young man who had gone to see Beaumont. He was unshaven, his khaki drills were only half buttoned and blotched with rifle oil and cartridge burns. But the biggest change was in his eyes. His eyes had seen terrible things, he was weary and had known failure. Yet he seemed more at ease with the world.

"Excuse me," Samuel said, "but why in the world do you smile?"

"Because," Remington said, pointing out to the

187

bush, "he is just like one of the bullies now. He's alone and for the first time, afraid."

Samuel thought about that for a moment. "Somehow," he said, "I don't think he's afraid of me."

They drank and silently watched the fire shoot sparks into the night air.

"I was just wondering if we will remember all this," Remington said.

"I could never forget Africa," Patterson said.

"You're young, Johnny," Remington said, taking a philosophical pull on his bottle. "So many things flash by, and at that moment we think, yes, this will stay with me. Surely I will never forget this dawn, this hunt, this passion." He shrugged. "But blink—it's gone." He looked at both Patterson and Samuel. "I hope it at least stays," he continued as he touched his forehead, "here."

Patterson toasted that with his bottle. "To memory." The others raised their bottles.

"I wanted to remember building the railroad," Samuel said. "Now I can't think why."

"Same for me about the bridge," Patterson said. He levered a thornbush limb on the fire. "But I can tell you the memory I wanted most: to see the birth of my son."

Remington stared at him across the fire, as though at the older brother he never saw grow up. Or at the father who died when he was way too young. "My life was shaped because someone invented gunpowder," he said. "It's taken me around the world, but the memory I wanted—that was the family I lost."

Patterson did a take, gave Remington a smirk, and

said, "You know, you're a very cheerful fellow when you drink."

Remington laughed and wrenched open another bottle of champagne. "When you meet your son," he said to Patterson, "hold him high." He raised the fresh bottle and drank in salute. He gave a courtly bow, turned, and went into his tent.

FIFTY-THREE

A train from the coast rolled into the Tsavo station
in the morning. The station master, the only British
civil servant in residence except for the telegrapher,
stood at his window and watched the passengers
disembark.

The station had an air of normality. Gone was the
feeling of an armed camp, gone too was the undertone
of terror that had accompanied arrivals and departures
for so many months.

A pretty Englishwoman stepped off the train carrying a bundle in her arms. She looked back and forth
and walked up to the window. "I'd like to see John
Patterson, please," she said.

Helena stood there in the Tsavo station smiling. She
looked weary from travel but still lovely in her white
dress. She held their son in her arms. The kid was
adorable.

She went on to the station master, "Could you tell
him that his wife—" She caught herself and started
over. "That his *family* has come to see him?"

Patterson was laboring at the bridge, doing a progress report and drawing up a new work schedule. The

190

bridge, only two-thirds finished, was inching forward again.

And once more, he had workers.

Deserters who had gone only as far as Voi had heard the news of the man-eater's death and were already flooding back into camp. Although another man-eater still ran free, somehow they believed the danger was over. They believed Patterson-*Sahib* had killed the Devil spirit and would protect them. They owed him allegiance, they had said, and they would accept whatever punishment he chose for their desertion.

"No punishment—work," was Patterson's simple prescription.

Now Samuel hurried to Patterson-*Sahib* with the stunning news from the station, and Patterson took off running.

At the station, the pretty picture of Helena in her long dress, walking with her sleeping baby in her arms, held the attention of onlookers. She walked back and forth along the shaded front of the building, no sounds in the air but the click of her heels on the timbers.

Patterson ran like crazy, up from the river, along the right of way, past the supply sheds, the big mess hut, the administration tent, across the blowing dusty field at the center of the settlement. He came in sight of the station.

Helena now saw him in the distance. She stepped out of the shadows of the station overhang, then walked out into the open at the end of the windy platform, smiling and waving excitedly.

Patterson caught sight of her and waved back excitedly.

191

The Darkness moved out of the grassy area across the tracks behind the station, coming up behind Helena and the child at an angle.

Patterson's eye immediately picked up the movement, and spotted the dark mane and the slow, rolling gait. He screamed, "Get back! *Back!*"

Helena was too far away, and his words were lost on the wind. She smiled and waved again, and moved further into the open.

Patterson was running now, waving his arms, screaming, *"Get back!"*

Helena still couldn't make out what he was saying, but all the same she stopped, looking out at him, not knowing to look around.

Behind her, the Darkness, low now, moved from shadow to shadow, donkey cart to tool shed to the shadow of the station itself, stalking silently, closing on the mother and the child.

The baby awoke and stretched adorably. Helena looked down at the infant and smiled. The baby mirrored his mother's wonderful smile.

The Darkness started to run from his crouch, now sprinting.

Patterson, still a hundred yards away, saw he was not going to get there in time.

Helena, now able to see Patterson's face at that distance, at last realized something was terribly wrong. She turned, but much too late. For as she turned, the Darkness made his running spring.

Patterson, unarmed, powerless, pounded in agony toward them.

The Darkness leapt upon the mother and child, took

them to the ground and ripped with his huge jaws as Helena cried out helplessly.

Patterson cried out in anguish. He threw his hands up, wrenched himself sideways as though to wrestle the beast away from his loved ones. He continued to cry out, thrashing, flailing, until he realized he was in his bed, in his tent, gripped by the most hideous nightmare a man could have.

He pulled himself up and tried to compose himself. Sweating, he stumbled out of his bed and over to his tent opening, throwing back the flap. He staggered outside.

It was dawn at Tsavo camp. Cool, clear air, pale blue sky, soft morning bird sounds. He moved out by the remains of the campfire, shaken, trying to rid his mind of the horrifying dream.

He looked around, to Samuel's tent at the front of the African village, then to Remington's tent to the right of Patterson's.

Then he saw: Remington's tent was ripped.

Patterson ran to it. The flap was closed, and the side of the tent bore a large vertical tear. He pushed through it and looked inside. It was empty. He looked around frantically and spotted blood on the tent floor.

FIFTY-FOUR

They ran, Patterson and Samuel, tracking as fast as they could, following the drag marks and the blood. Patterson had his eyes on the ground, on the bush ahead, and on the ravine that cut away from the river to the northwest. He ran with his finger wrapped around the trigger of his .303 carbine.

Samuel ran with him, also carrying a rifle, scrambling to keep up.

Patterson, wild-eyed, led them through the ravine, splashing through the small river at the bottom of it. He gestured for them to split up on the other side, widening the area of search. Samuel veered off, skirting the tall papyrus reeds along the shore.

Patterson plunged ahead into a thorn thicket. He charged through, unmindful of the damage to his clothes and the ripping of his skin. He scanned around, searching while he ran, cutting through more thorn scrub.

A strange shadow loomed on his left. He spun toward it, rifle ready, and advanced, taking deep breaths.

He moved around an impenetrable brake and looked. Nothing at all.

Just his imagination, which was working hard, generating possibilities, hope. Nothing was there. No signs even, no more tracks. He looked around, unsure where to go, what to do.

Then a voice came on the wind—*"Sahib!"*—at a little distance. Samuel's voice calling to him.

Patterson tracked the direction of the sound.

Samuel's voice cried out again, louder.

Patterson started to run and run, out of the thorn forest, past the sandy bottom along the papyrus reeds, toward Samuel's voice. He breasted a rise at the edge of a field with tall green grass bowing and rippling with the morning breeze.

Yards out in the middle of the grass, opposite the far end of the bridge, he saw Samuel's shoulders and head, looking down.

Patterson ran toward him, his rifle ready. Samuel's head and shoulders sank out of sight. Patterson ran straight for him until he came to the spot.

In the middle of the pale green grass was a patch that was blood red.

Samuel rose from the blood-red patch in shock and in despair. He had seen something beyond even his hardened imagination.

Patterson looked down into the blood-red grass and saw Remington, clearly dead. But it was more than just that. The body was badly dismembered—not eaten, just torn asunder, ripped, thrown wide, again and again. It was a picture of fury so intense, it looked like the work of a pride of lions, or a pack of wild dogs.

But around the body were the pugs of just one lion. Just the Darkness.

Patterson and Samuel stared mutely at the ground. Patterson bent and picked something out of the grass. Remington's double-barreled pistol. It hadn't been fired. He wiped the blood from its barrel.

FIFTY-FIVE

In late afternoon, when the shadows were long, Patterson and Samuel were ready.

They had gathered Remington's remains, in the place where they found him, and wrapped him in the pale green grasses. They pulled dried grasses from the ground, built a bier, and placed him on it. They pulled more grasses up by the roots and laid them over and around him. They worked until the grass was piled high on his body.

Patterson said a Christian prayer and recited a verse he knew by heart from the Bible, from Isaiah. "Those who wait on the Lord shall renew their strength. They shall mount up with wings like eagles. They shall run and not be weary. They shall walk and not faint."

Samuel recited an Akamba chant. They lit their torches and fired the grass pyre.

Now they stared into the flames that rose in the darkening sky.

Samuel, accustomed to the frequency of early and violent deaths in his land, was still having a hard time holding himself together.

They stood like statues as the flames consumed the grassy monument they'd constructed.

They performed Remington's funeral ceremony alone. Only they weren't alone.

A roar from the deep chest of the Darkness erupted behind them, deafening, triumphant, shaking the ground.

The man-eater was between them and the bridge. The lion had the men cut off. He could stalk them at leisure, then wreak his revenge.

Patterson saw the deadly positioning and just as quickly saw a way to reverse the advantage.

He suddenly started to move. He was running, carrying a torch. Samuel wasn't sure what he was doing. Then it became clear. He was lighting the grassy field, spreading the fire in the oncoming darkness. The flames crackled and roared, licking at the sky. They formed a crescent around the lion, a red fiery wall.

Now it was the Darkness who had his back up against it. His prey disappeared in the sensory overload. The fire blinded the lion's acute senses of smell and hearing. The flames obscured the men's movements.

Behind the flames, Samuel rejoined Patterson and handed him Remington's rifle. They turned toward the lion. This would be it. Armageddon was about to happen, the end was here, one way or another.

On the other side of the flames, it appeared the whole horizon was on fire. The sky was as bright as if by lightning. The lion backed toward the bridge.

Just as the Darkness turned and moved out on the bridge, Patterson came exploding through the flames, firing his carbine. The Darkness was hit. He roared horribly and went down.

Patterson turned to Samuel right behind him, reached for his rifle, grabbed it, and turned back, ready to fire again.

The Darkness was gone.

Patterson and Samuel looked around. The man-eater had simply disappeared. "Where is it?" Patterson asked, confused.

Samuel pointed down. "Underneath," he said. "Somewhere."

FIFTY-SIX

Below them, where Samuel was pointing, was the su-
perstructure of the bridge. The bolted iron and wood
latticework ran several levels down from where the
rail bed would be.

Below them, where Samuel was pointing, was the su-
perstructure of the bridge. The bolted iron and wood
latticework ran several levels down from where the
rail bed would be.

They looked at each other and saw the bad news.
There were dozens of places to hide. Worse still, there
were many crevices, gaps, and holes connecting the
spaces below with the open space above. Countless
numbers of holes.

Patterson and Samuel stepped onto the end of the
bridge where construction began. The unfinished
structure stretched seventy feet in the air before them.
They started carefully forward.

As they moved along, they peered down cautiously
through every gap and crevice they came to. Making
sure they missed nothing.

Samuel was terrified, holding his single-shot rifle extremely tight. His dangling, decorated earlobes clicked
as he spun his head, looking here and there. This was
not his idea of how to deal with a lion, especially a
crazed man-eater such as this. The rage of a lion was

a terrible thing of nature. A sane man didn't walk into its embrace if there was any other choice.

But Patterson was not now sane. He had thrown aside all other considerations save vengeance. Vengeance for Starling, Remington, Mahina, and the hundred other Indian coolies and stonemasons and tribesmen and Englishmen in his employ who had had hideous deaths in the jaws of the two beasts. Vengeance too for the humiliation and terror they had visited on his soul, making him know forever he was no powerful warrior, only a frightened rabbit.

To say it had become personal for him was hugely understating it. This lion *was* him—his own fear and irresolution, his own dullwittedness and complacency in the face of an animal's searing purity of purpose. This was the thing he had to overpower so he could look his son in the eye one day and say, as fathers long to say, "Grow up like me."

There were some holes up ahead in the roadbed. The nearest one was also the largest. The two men slowed and approached in silence, guns ready, trying to see what was in there.

The hole seemed empty.

Patterson and Samuel froze, listening. They expected to hear panting, the heavy liquid breathing of a wounded cat. But they heard nothing.

Patterson got low and peered into the shadowy interior at every angle. He saw nothing. Samuel looked this way and that, covering their rear. Patterson straightened up, half turned to move on to the next hiding place.

The Darkness just came flying out of the hole in all his immensity with a noise like the wrath of God.

Patterson fell backward and fired, and the Darkness, airborne over him like a mountain, was hit. He veered slightly and went down and rolled on his side, then started to right himself.

Patterson turned to grab Samuel's rifle from him. Only Samuel wasn't there.

Samuel had taken off for the trees at the end of the bridge.

The Darkness was up and roaring, and Patterson, without turning to look, took off too, running across the half-completed, crevice-filled bridge as fast as he could pick his way without slipping off or falling or breaking a leg.

Samuel made it to the end of the bridge and jumped for the branch of the nearest tree and scrambled way up.

The Darkness, gut-wounded, loped after Patterson with huge strides, eating up the distance between them.

Patterson ran for his life, burning up the span of the bridge, trying to escape.

The Darkness, with his sprinting speed, would already have run Patterson down and crushed the vertebrae of his neck with one life-ending clamp of jaws. But wounded, limping, he was slower. But he was still faster than Patterson, and still closing fast.

Patterson, running faster than ever before in his life, was hearing the lion's raging growl grow louder, closer. He could feel the colossal weight come crashing down on his back at any second.

He sprang into the air and with both hands grabbed a branch of the tree next to the one that Samuel had

202

climbed. He swung his legs up with desperate strength and lifted his body up into the boughs just as the Darkness launched himself, making a powerful cut with his razored forepaw, just missing.

Patterson got his body onto a branch and almost fell from just the might of the roar that erupted from the Darkness. The great beast, thundering in psychotic fury, paced in quick steps below, capable of any insane act that would get him this prey.

Samuel, clutching his rifle, climbed higher into his tree.

Patterson climbed higher in his, until he was eighteen feet up.

The lion circled the trunk of Patterson's tree raging with frustration, his huge black-maned mug staring up, baring stark white fangs against pitch-black lips.

Patterson, exhausted but feeling safe up this high, feeling a respite from the terror, breathed easier. He looked across at the next tree and gave Samuel a relieved look.

Samuel shrugged, embarrassed. "Afraid of lions," he said.

Patterson nodded. "It's all right, Samuel," he said. "We all get hit. . . ." Then he shut up fast.

FIFTY-SEVEN

Patterson shut up fast because the Darkness was doing something he did not believe. Lions are cats, and when cats want to climb, up they go. And that's what the Darkness was now driven to, with these simians chattering, mocking him up above, so close.

He dug into the broad trunk of the tree with his hind legs pushing him up, embracing the trunk with his powerful forelegs, clawing upward foot by foot.

Patterson instinctively reached for the branch above and climbed higher, terrified anew, adrenaline coursing, heart thudding painfully in his chest.

The lion just kept coming, past the first big fork, climbing, one foreclaw ahead of the other.

Patterson mounted higher. The whole tree began shaking as the five-hundred-pound monster pulled itself up toward him. The lion was breathing so loud and so close Patterson thought he might faint.

Patterson went higher still and the branches were getting thinner and he was swaying as the lion shook the tree with his tremendous weight. Patterson felt the branches bending. He could fall, they could break.

The Darkness climbed on. Nothing could stop him.

Patterson was at the limit. No more branches would support his weight. The lion came slower now, picking for sturdy footing but still coming.

Patterson turned and called out. "Samuel!" He gestured frantically for Samuel's single-shot rifle.

Samuel took his rifle between his two hands and, watching the lion crawling inexorably up toward Patterson's legs, tossed the weapon with great care across the fifteen-foot gap.

It was a good throw, and Patterson reached out, hands positioned to catch it and cradle it in. But the rifle, in midair, sailing just so toward Patterson's outstretched hands, just barely ticked a tree branch and spun away to the ground.

The Darkness, so near that Patterson could smell his fetid moist breath rising around him, lunged his vast weight upward the last few feet and swiped out with his scimitar claws. Patterson jumped.

Without thinking, he just leapt out of the tree—twenty-some feet—too far down to expect an undamaged landing. But he had run out of good choices, and the only ones left were bad or worse.

Samuel watched him plummet and land hard on the packed earth around the tree. He lay stunned, unmoving, ribs broken, leg cracked, breath knocked out. He thought he was dying.

But then Death itself came wildly scrambling down the tree, snapping branches, looking for room to turn his great mass around.

Patterson crawled for the rifle on the ground. In terrible pain, he reached for it, grabbed it, and turned as the Darkness came skittering and crashing down the trunk of the tree, hitting the ground.

Patterson forced himself to his feet. With a growing roar, the Darkness started at him with a stalking gait, then quickly accelerated into a full charge.

Patterson fired the small rifle. The Darkness, hit in the neck, went down, but it wasn't enough. He clawed the dust into a spray as he scrambled to his feet and came on again.

Patterson pulled out Remington's double-barreled pistol and fired the final shot point-blank.

The Darkness, hit again, vomiting blood, had to stop. Lung punctured, aorta pierced, pelvis fractured, he *had* to go down. But still he didn't. He kept coming.

No place to hide, all bullets gone, all Patterson could do with his cracked leg and busted ribs was try to back up. He managed one step backward, fell over a thick fallen branch, and landed hard. He watched the majestic ruined lion move toward him, framed between his splayed legs. Six feet away, now four.

The giant yellow eyes gleamed pure hatred for the man, and the beast lunged downward with his great jaws and, going to the ground, buried his teeth in the thick fallen branch. He bit through it with the last of his enormous strength and, with a long sigh, died.

Patterson couldn't breathe.

The Darkness, the black-maned devil, lay before him dead, lifeless eyes staring, his teeth still buried in the tree branch.

Patterson sat back, waiting for the adrenaline tremor to pass. He took a deep breath and suddenly just emptied. He let go, tears poured down his face. He began to cry out loud, his body wracked with sobs.

He managed to crawl to his knees and move next to the animal. The gigantic evil face was now at rest, the flying nightmarish black mane now limp, bloody, and dirt-caked.

Samuel, climbing gingerly down from the tree, could hear just the sound of Patterson's exhausted sobs.

FIFTY-EIGHT

The sun shone on the seventy-yard bridge across the hundred-yard gorge.

Patterson stood alone out on the end that yearned for the far shore. It was now going to get there.

Patterson looked pretty good again. But not good in the way he did when he came out to Africa. He was unshaven still, and he wore Remington's handmade buffalo-hide coat. In his stance and demeanor, he looked more like Remington than his old self.

Samuel, with his tall staff back in his hands instead of a gun, stood up on the high bank of the river. His eyes were tired, but his posture was relaxed for the first time in many months. The job facing him was a hard one, but not an impossible one. All he had to do now was oversee his temperamental workers bringing new material by donkey cart onto the bridge, and make sure they worked more than squabbled with each other.

As Samuel was watching, a young Englishman hurried out the span toward Patterson.

The young man, reminiscent of Starling in his lean form and energetic manner, stopped before Patterson and spoke deferentially. "Colonel?" the young man said. "I'm Nigel Bransford, here to replace Angus Starling."

Patterson shook Bransford's proffered hand.

Clearly impressed, Bransford said, "So proud to meet you, Patterson the Lion Killer. I do wish I'd been here for the hunt."

"No you don't," Patterson said, looking away—looking out across the endless bushland that harbored memories of horrors.

Samuel stepped out onto the bridge bearing a message a runner had handed to him. He approached Patterson and spoke to him in Swahili. "John, *samahani. Wageni wako,*" he said. "John, excuse me. You have visitors."

Patterson answered briefly in Swahili and hurried away down the length of the bridge and up the bank. *"Mtoto wangu?"* he said to himself. "My child?"

He crossed into the central settlement of Tsavo and headed across the dusty open stretch in the middle.

Coming toward him from the station with his bundle of belongings and tools was a familiar scowling figure in a brick red turban. Abdullah, the Indian headman who had fled with the others at the height of the panic.

All around Abdullah, more workers were streaming from the station, more returnees ready to take up their posts, hoping for their rupee bonuses despite all that had happened.

Abdullah and Patterson looked at each other as they approached. Finally Abdullah nodded in respect. Patterson nodded back. They passed each other without speaking.

Patterson focused on the train platform in the distance. There stood Helena with a child in her arms, in exactly the same pose she'd had in Patterson's nightmare. Patterson froze.

But this was not a nightmare. Helena waved and smiled. Patterson broke into a run and went to her. He took her in her arms and embraced her.

She handed him their son.

Patterson looked at the boy a moment and then held him high over his head, staring up at him, turning and turning around with him in the equatorial sunshine.

EPILOGUE

People came back, Patterson finished the bridge, then people went their ways.

Samuel stood in an elevated place looking out over the burned grassy field—grown tall and green now—toward the west, toward the Great Rift Valley and the Kikuyu Hills and the railroad's terminus at Ugowe Bay on Lake Victoria beyond.

Those like Samuel who stayed still wondered. How did the lions escape for nine months? And kill 135 men? And stop the railroad?

And were they only lions?

Samuel walked along the elevated path toward the field of struggle, drawn there as he often was this time of day.

A gold and scarlet sunset streaked the west, then began fading into the intense violet of a beautiful, mild African evening.

Samuel stepped down from the elevated path and walked into the grass, his tall staff his only companion.

Turning, he looked back at the path he had just walked and admired it. Patterson's stone and steel bridge. *His* bridge too. The bridge of all those who lived and all those who died building it.

It was a handsome structure. Three strong carved-stone piers, giant steel girders, solid webbed spans to withstand the heavy freight of soldiers and civilization now pouring into Africa's interior.

The native tribes and the animals backed off a little from the machines and men who came on the iron rails of civilization, wondering what their coming meant.

Samuel had an inkling what it meant, and yet he didn't despair. He walked out on the grassy plain, on quiet, peaceful evenings with a little breeze blowing, and he didn't frown for the fate of his invaded land, he smiled. Africa was the most resilient of lands; this much he knew.

The barest breeze stirred. The tall grass heads bent and a green ripple flowed across the vast field.

Samuel walked on, with only his staff as companion.

A tail flicked in the tall grass.

Were they only lions, the Ghost and the Darkness?

If you want to decide for yourself, you must go to America. They are there, at the Field Museum in Chicago. And even now, after they have been dead a century, if you dare to lock eyes with them, you will be afraid.

Sleep well.